9×p

1000

Selected by ROBERT HASS

CZESLAW

SELECTED

POEMS

1931–2004

MILOSZ

Foreword by SEAMUS HEANEY

HarperCollins books may be purchased for educational, business,
or sales promotional use. For information, please write: Special Markets Department,
HarperCollins Publishers, 10 East 53rd Street, New York, NY 10022.

"Watering Can," "From My Dentist's Window," and "Rivers" from *Road-side Dog*
by Czeslaw Milosz, copyright © 1998 by Czeslaw Milosz; reprinted by permission
of Farrar, Straus and Giroux, LLC.

"The Door Stands Open," by Seamus Heaney, copyright © 2004 by Seamus Heaney,
originally appeared in *The New Republic,* September 13, 2004.

FIRST EDITION

Designed by Kate Nichols

The Library of Congress Cataloging-in-Publication Data has been applied for.

ISBN-10: 0-06-018867-7
ISBN-13: 978-0-06-018867-2

06 07 08 09 10 NMSG/QF 10 9 8 7 6 5 4 3 2 1

CONTENTS

A NOTE ON THE TEXTS AND THEIR SELECTION

Czeslaw Milosz published a *Selected Poems* in 1973 with Seabury Press. It was the volume that introduced him to English-speaking readers and it was republished, with some small revisions by the author, by Ecco Press in 1980. This was supplanted by *The Collected Poems* of 1988, an almost complete selection of the poems of his that had been translated into English at that time. That book was followed by *New and Collected Poems, 1931–2001,* a nearly complete collection of all his poems that had been translated into English. It drew upon *Poezje,* the three volume edition of his poems published in Paris by Instytut Literacki in 1981–82 and the several individual Polish volumes that were published between 1982 and 2001. *New and Collected Poems* included all of the poems of Milosz published in English that he wished to keep in print, except for those in his final book, *A Second Space* (Ecco Press, 2003).

This volume uses the English texts from *New and Collected Poems, 1931–2001* and *A Second Space,* 2003, except for "A Song on the End of the World," which is a newly revised translation by Anton Milosz.

In the last years of his life two volumes of selections of Milosz's poems in Polish appeared under his supervision, *Wiersze Wybrane,* Panstwowy Instytut Wydawniczy, Warsaw, 1996, and a bilingual *Poezje Wybrane/Selected Poems,* Wydawnictwo Literackie, Krakow, 1996. This selection was made with an eye to the selections made by the editors of those volumes, which were approved by the author.

The poems are dated and arranged by year of composition through 1986, following Milosz's dating of the poems in the *New and Collected.*

Thereafter they are arranged in the order in which they appeared in subsequent English volumes. Two of the longer poems, "A Treatise on Poetry" and "From the Rising of the Sun," are excerpted here. The brief selection from "A Treatise on Poetry" is the one made from that book-length poem by the author for his *Collected Poems* of 1988 and the version of "From the Rising of the Sun" also follows that volume by excluding, "Lauda," a long section of the poem dealing with the history of Lithuania. It can be found in the *New and Selected Poems.*

Thanks to Adam Zagajewski and Robert Faggen and Daniel Halpern for their help with the final selections for this volume. (RH)

THE DOOR STANDS OPEN

by Seamus Heaney

FOR QUITE A WHILE NOW, those who knew Czeslaw Milosz couldn't help wondering what it was going to be like when he was gone. In the meantime he more than held his own, writing away for all he was worth in Kraków, in his early nineties, in an apartment where I had the privilege of visiting him twice. On the first occasion he was confined to his bed, too unwell to attend a conference arranged in his honor, and on the second he was ensconced in his living room, face-to-face with a life-size bronze head and torso of his second wife, Carol. His junior by some thirty years, she had died from a quick and cruel cancer in 2002, and as he sat on one side of the room facing the bronze on the other, the old poet seemed to be viewing it and everything else from another shore. On that occasion he was being ministered to by his daughter-in-law, and perhaps it was her hovering attentions as much as his translated appearance that brought to mind the aged Oedipus being minded by daughters in the grove at Colonus, the old king who had arrived where he knew he would die. Colonus was not his birthplace, but it was where he had come home to himself, to the world, and to the otherworld; and the same could be said of Milosz in Kraków.

"The child who dwells inside us trusts that there are wise men somewhere who know the truth": so Milosz had written, and for his many friends he himself was one of those wise men. His sayings were quoted, even when they were wisecracks rather than wisdom. A few days before he died I had a letter from Robert Pinsky, telling of a visit the previous month to the hospital where Czeslaw was a patient. "How are you?" Robert asked. "Conscious," was the reply. "My head is full of absurd bric-a-brac." It was the first time I had ever detected a daunted note in any of his utterances. A couple of years earlier, for example, a similar inquiry from Robert Hass had elicited the reply "I survive by incantation"—which was more like him. His life and works were founded upon faith in "A word wakened by lips that perish."

This first artistic principle was clearly related to the last Gospel of the Mass, the *In principio* of St. John: "In the beginning was the Word." Inexorably then, through his pursuit of poetic vocation, his study of what such pursuit entailed, and the unremitting, abounding yield of his habit of composition, he developed a fierce conviction about the holy force of his art, how poetry was called upon to combat death and nothingness, to be "A tireless messenger who runs and runs/Through interstellar fields, through the revolving galaxies,/And calls out, protests, screams" ("Meaning"). With Milosz gone, the world has lost a credible witness to this immemorial belief in the saving power of poetry.

His credibility was and remains the thing. There was nothing disingenuous about Milosz's professions of faith in poetry, which he once called philosophy's "ally in the service of the good," news that "was brought to the mountains by a unicorn and an echo." Such trust in the delicious joy-bringing potential of art and intellect was protected by strong bulwarks built from the knowledge and experience that he had gained at first hand and at great cost. His mind, to put it another way, was at once a garden—now a monastery garden, now a garden of earthly delights—and a citadel. The fortifications surrounding the garden were situated on a high mountain whence he could view the kingdoms of the world, recognize their temptations and their tragedies, and communicate to his readers both the airiness and the insights that his situation afforded. In one of his poems he compares a poem to a bridge built out of air over air, and one of the great delights of his work is a corresponding sensation of invigilating reality from a head-clearing perspective, being liberated into the authentic solitude of one's own being and at the same time being given gratifyingly spiritual companionship, so that one is ready to say something like "It is good for us to be here."

Milosz was well aware of this aspect of his work and explicit about his wish that poetry in general should be capable of providing such an elevated plane of regard. Yet as if to prove the truth of Blake's contention that without contrarieties there could be no progression, he was equally emphatic about poetry's need to descend from its high vantage point and creep about among the nomads on the plain. It was not enough that the poet should be like Thetis in Auden's poem "The Shield of Achilles," looking over the shoulder of his artifact at a far-off panorama that included everything from kitchen comedy to genocide. The poet had to be down there with the ordinary crowd, at eye level with the refugee family on the floor of the railway station, sharing the smell of the stale crusts that the mother is doling out to her youngsters even as the boots of the military patrol bear down on them, the city is bombarded, and maps and memories go up in flames.

Awareness of the triteness and the tribulations of other people's lives was needed to humanize the song. It was not enough to be in the salons of the avant-garde. Certain things, as he says in "1945," could not be learned "from Apollinaire,/Or Cubist manifestos, or the festivals of Paris streets." Milosz would have deeply understood and utterly agreed with Keats's contention that the use of a world of pain and troubles was to school the intelligence and make it a soul. The discharged soldier of "1945" has received just such schooling:

> On the steppe, as he was binding his bleeding feet with a rag
> He grasped the futile pride of those lofty generations.
> As far as he could see, a flat, unredeemed earth.

And what, in these drastic conditions, has the poet to offer? Only what has accrued to him through custom and ceremony, through civilization:

> I blinked, ridiculous and rebellious,
> Alone with my Jesus Mary against irrefutable power,
> A descendant of ardent prayers, of gilded sculptures and miracles.

Tender toward innocence, tough-minded when faced with brutality and injustice, Milosz could be at one moment susceptible, at another remorseless. Now he is evoking the dewy eroticism of some adolescent girl haunting the grounds of a Lithuanian manor house, now he is anatomizing the traits of character and misdirected creative gifts that led some of his contemporaries into the Marxist web. From start to finish, merciless analytic power coexisted with helpless sensuous relish. He recollects the fresh bread smells on the streets of Paris when he was a student at the same moment as he summons up the faces of fellow students from Indochina, young revolutionaries preparing to seize power and "kill in the name of the universal beautiful ideas."

No doubt the intensity of his early religious training contributed to his capacity to let perpetual light shine upon the quotidian, yet this religious poet was inhabited by another who was, in a very precise sense, a secular Milosz, one afflicted by the atrociousness of the *saeculum* he was fated to live through. The word "century," usually preceded by the definite article or the possessive pronoun, first-person singular, repeats and echoes all through his writing. It was as if he couldn't go anywhere without encountering, as he does in his poem "A Treatise on Poetry," "The Spirit of History . . . out walking," wearing "About his neck a chain of severed heads." And it was his face-to-face encounters and contentions with this "inferior god" that darkened his understanding and endowed everything he wrote with grievous force.

His intellectual life could be viewed as a long single combat with shape-shifting untruth. "The New Faith" upon which the communist regimes were founded was like the old man of the sea, a villainous fallacious Proteus who had to be watched, wrestled with, held down, and made to submit. Just how much stamina and precision this entailed can be seen in the almost inquisitorial prosecution of argument and accusation that characterizes *The Captive Mind,* the book that he introduced like a bell and candle between himself and his Polish contemporaries who had succumbed to the Marxist tempters. The sense of personal majesty that developed around him in old age derived in no small measure from his having survived this ordeal, which sprung him into solitude and left him a wanderer, as capable in the end of self-accusation as he had been of accusation.

SELECTED POEMS

1931–2004

DAWNS

A tall building. The walls crept upward in the dark,
Above the rustle of maple leaves, above hurrying feet.
A tall building, dawning with its lights above the square.
Inside hissing softly in the predawn hours,
The elevator moved between the floors. The cables twanged.
A rooster's cry rang in the pipes and gutters
Till a shiver ran through the house. Those awakened heard
This singing in the walls, terrible as the earth's happiness.

Already the screech of a tram. And day. And smoke again.
Oh, the day is dark. Above us, who are shut
High up in our rooms, flocks of birds
Fly by in a whir of flickering wings.
Not enough. One life is not enough.
I'd like to live twice on this sad planet,
In lonely cities, in starved villages,
To look at all evil, at the decay of bodies,
And probe the laws to which the time was subject,
Time that howled above us like a wind.

In the courtyard of the apartment house street musicians
Croon in chorus. The hands of listeners shine at the windows.
She gets up from her rumpled sheets.
In her dreams she thought of dresses and travel.
She walks up to the black mirror. Youth didn't last long.
Nobody knew that work would divide a day
Into great toil and dead rest,
And that the moon would pause every spring
Above the sleep of the weary ones. In our hearts' heavy beating
No spring for us anymore, nor love.

To cover up one's thighs. Let them not,
With their lacing of thin purple veins, remember
This child rushing down the staircase,

This child running down the gray sidewalk.
Laughter can still be heard in the distance—
Anew, everything the child will discover anew
And down an immense, empty, frosty road
Through a space ringing with the thunder of the pulse
Her child will go. And time will howl.
Standing naked in front of her mirror, the woman
Lightly wipes away two tears with her kerchief
And darkens her eyebrows with henna.

Wilno, 1932

THE SONG

Earth flows away from the shore where I stand,
her trees and grasses, more and more distant, shine.
Buds of chestnuts, lights of frail birches,
I won't see you anymore.
With worn-out people you move away,
with the sun waving like a flag you run toward the night,
I am afraid to stay here alone, I have nothing except my body
—it glistens in the dark, a star with crossed hands,
so that I am scared to look at myself. Earth,
do not abandon me.

CHORUS:
Ice flowed down the rivers, trees sprouted buoyant leaves,
ploughs went through the fields, doves in the forest are cooing,
a doe runs in the hills and cries her exulting songs,
tall-stemmed flowers are blooming, steam rises from warm gardens,
Children throw balls, they dance on the meadow by threesomes,
women wash linen at streamside and fish for the moon.
All joy comes from the earth, there is no delight without her,
man is given to the earth, let him desire no other.

WOMAN:
I don't want you, don't tempt me, keep flowing, my tranquil sister.
Your burning touch on my neck, I still feel it.
Nights of love with you bitter as the ash of clouds,
and the dawn after them, red, and on the lakes
first terns circling and such sadness
that I could not cry anymore, just keep counting
the hours of the morning, listen to the cold rustle
of the high, dead poplars. You, God, have mercy on me.
From the earth's greedy mouth deliver me,
cleanse me of her untrue songs.

CHORUS:

The capstans are turning, fish toss in the nets,
baked breads smell sweetly, apples roll on the tables,
evenings go down the steps and the steps are live flesh—
everything is begot by the earth, she is without blemish.
Heavy ships are yawing, copper brethren are sailing,
animals sway their backs, butterflies fall to the sea,
baskets wander at dusk, dawn lives in the apple tree—
everything is begot by the earth, to her everything will return.

WOMAN:

Oh, if there were in me one seed without rust,
no more than one grain that could perdure,
I could sleep in the cradle leaning by turns
now into darkness, now into the break of day.
I would wait quietly till the slow movement ceases
and the real shows itself naked suddenly,
till a wildflower, a stone in the fields stare up
with the disk of an unknown new face.
Then they who live in the lies
like weeds at the bottom of a bay's wash
would only be what pine needles are
when one looks from above through the clouds at a forest.
But there is nothing in me, just fear,
nothing but the running of dark waves.
I am the wind that blows and dies out in dark waters,
I am the wind going and not returning,
a milkweed pollen on the black meadows of the world.

THE LAST VOICES:

At the forge on the lake shore, hammerblows,
a man, bent over, fixes a scythe,
his head gleams in the flame of the hearth.

A resin chip is lit in the hut,
tired ploughboys lay their heads on the table.
A bowl is already steaming and the crickets sing.

Islands are animals falling asleep,
in the nest of the lake they settle down, purring:
above them, a narrow cloud.

Wilno, 1934

SLOW RIVER

There has not been for a long time a spring
as beautiful as this one; the grass, just before mowing,
is thick and wet with dew. At night bird cries
come up from the edge of the marsh, a crimson shoal
lies in the east till the morning hours.
In such a season, every voice becomes for us
a shout of triumph. Glory, pain and glory
to the grass, to the clouds, to the green oak wood.
The gates of the earth torn open, the key
to the earth revealed. A star is greeting the day.
Then why do your eyes hold an impure gleam
like the eyes of those who have not tasted
evil and long only for crime? Why does this heat
and depth of hatred radiate
from your narrowed eyes? To you the rule,
for you clouds in golden rings
play a music, maples by the road exalt you.
The invisible rein on every living thing
leads to your hand—pull, and they all
turn a half-circle under the canopy
called cirrus. And your tasks? A wooded mountain
awaits you, the place for cities in the air,
a valley where wheat should grow, a table, a white page
on which, maybe, a long poem could be started,
joy and toil. And the road bolts like an animal,
it falls away so quickly, leaving a trail of dust,
that there is scarcely a sight to prepare a nod for,
the hand's grip already weakened, a sigh, and the storm is over.
And then they carry the malefactor through the fields,
rocking his gray head, and above the seashore
on a tree-lined avenue, they put him down
where the wind from the bay furls banners

and schoolchildren run on the gravel paths,
singing their songs.

—"So that neighing in the gardens, drinking on the green,
so that, not knowing whether they are happy or just weary,
they take bread from the hands of their pregnant wives.
They bow their heads to nothing in their lives.
My brothers, avid for pleasure, smiling, beery,
have the world for a granary, a house of joy."

—"Ah, dark rabble at their vernal feasts
and crematoria rising like white cliffs
and smoke seeping from the dead wasps' nests.
In a stammer of mandolins, a dust-cloud of scythes,
on heaps of food and mosses stomped ash-gray,
the new sun rises on another day."

For a long time there has not been a spring
as beautiful as this one to the voyager.
The expanse of water seems to him dense
as the blood of hemlock. And a fleet of sails
speeding in the dark, like the last
vibration of a pure note. He saw
human figures scattered on the sands
under the light of planets, falling from the vault
of heaven, and when a wave grew silent, it was silent,
the foam smelled of iodine? heliotrope?
They sang on the dunes, Maria, Maria,
resting a spattered hand on the saddle
and he didn't know if this was the new sign
that promises salvation, but kills first.
Three times must the wheel of blindness

turn, before I look without fear at the power
sleeping in my own hand, and recognize spring,
the sky, the seas, and the dark, massed land.
Three times will the liars have conquered
before the great truth appears alive
and in the splendor of one moment
stand spring and the sky, the seas, the lands.

Wilno, 1936

ENCOUNTER

We were riding through frozen fields in a wagon at dawn.
A red wing rose in the darkness.

And suddenly a hare ran across the road.
One of us pointed to it with his hand.

That was long ago. Today neither of them is alive,
Not the hare, nor the man who made the gesture.

O my love, where are they, where are they going—
The flash of a hand, streak of movement, rustle of pebbles.
I ask not out of sorrow, but in wonder.

Wilno, 1936

A BOOK IN THE RUINS

A dark building. Crossed boards, nailed up, create
A barrier at the entrance, or a gate
When you go in. Here, in the gutted foyer,
The ivy snaking down the walls is wire
Dangling. And over there the twisted metal
Columns rising from the undergrowth of rubble
Are tattered tree trunks. This could be the brick
Of the library, you don't know yet, or the sick
Grove of dry white aspen where, stalking birds,
You met a Lithuanian dusk stirred
From its silence only by the wails of hawks.
Now walk carefully. You see whole blocks
Of ceiling caved in by a recent blast.
And above, through jagged tiers of plaster,
A patch of blue. Pages of books lying
Scattered at your feet are like fern-leaves hiding
A moldy skeleton, or else fossils
Whitened by the secrets of Jurassic shells.
A remnant life so ancient and unknown
Compels a scientist, tilting a stone
Into the light, to wonder. He can't know
Whether it is some dead epoch's shadow
Or a living form. He looks again
At chalk spirals eroded by the rain,
The rust of tears. Thus, in a book picked up
From the ruins, you see a world erupt
And glitter with its distant sleepy past,
Green times of creatures tumbled to the vast
Abyss and backward: the brows of women,
An earring fixed with trembling hand, pearl button
On a glove, candelabra in the mirror.
The lanterns have been lit. A first shiver
Passes over the instruments. The quadrille
Begins to curl, subdued by the rustle

Of big trees swaying in the formal park.
She slips outside, her shawl floating in the dark,
And meets him in a bower overgrown
With vines. They sit close on a bench of stone
And watch the lanterns glowing in the jasmine.
Or here, this stanza: you hear a goose pen
Creak, the butterfly of an oil lamp
Flutters slowly over scrolls and parchment,
A crucifix, bronze busts. The lines complain,
In plangent rhythms, that desire is vain.
Here a city rises. In the market square
Signboards clang, a stagecoach rumbles in to scare
A flock of pigeons up. Under the town clock,
In the tavern, a hand pauses in the stock
Gesture of arrest—meanwhile workers walk
Home from the textile mill, townsfolk talk
On the steps—and the hand moves now to evoke
The fire of justice, a world gone up in smoke,
The voice quavering with the revenge of ages.
So the world seems to drift from these pages
Like the mist clearing on a field at dawn.
Only when two times, two forms are drawn
Together and their legibility
Disturbed, do you see that immortality
Is not very different from the present
And is for its sake. You pick a fragment
Of grenade which pierced the body of a song
On Daphnis and Chloe. And you long,
Ruefully, to have a talk with her,
As if it were what life prepared you for.
—How is it, Chloe, that your pretty skirt
Is torn so badly by the winds that hurt
Real people, you who, in eternity, sing
The hours, sun in your hair appearing

And disappearing? How is it that your breasts
Are pierced by shrapnel, and the oak groves burn,
While you, charmed, not caring at all, turn
To run through forests of machinery and concrete
And haunt us with the echoes of your feet?
If there is such an eternity, lush
Though short-lived, that's enough. But how . . . hush!
We were predestined to live when the scene
Grows dim and the outline of a Greek ruin
Blackens the sky. It is noon, and wandering
Through a dark building, you see workers sitting
Down to a fire a narrow ray of sunlight
Kindles on the floor. They have dragged out
Heavy books and made a table of them
And begun to cut their bread. In good time
A tank will clatter past, a streetcar chime.

Warsaw, 1941

CAMPO DEI FIORI

In Rome on the Campo dei Fiori
baskets of olives and lemons,
cobbles spattered with wine
and the wreckage of flowers.
Vendors cover the trestles
with rose-pink fish;
armfuls of dark grapes
heaped on peach-down.

On this same square
they burned Giordano Bruno.
Henchmen kindled the pyre
close-pressed by the mob.
Before the flames had died
the taverns were full again,
baskets of olives and lemons
again on the vendors' shoulders.

I thought of the Campo dei Fiori
in Warsaw by the sky-carousel
one clear spring evening
to the strains of a carnival tune.
The bright melody drowned
the salvos from the ghetto wall,
and couples were flying
high in the cloudless sky.

At times wind from the burning
would drift dark kites along
and riders on the carousel
caught petals in midair.
That same hot wind
blew open the skirts of the girls

and the crowds were laughing
on that beautiful Warsaw Sunday.

Someone will read as moral
that the people of Rome or Warsaw
haggle, laugh, make love
as they pass by martyrs' pyres.
Someone else will read
of the passing of things human,
of the oblivion
born before the flames have died.

But that day I thought only
of the loneliness of the dying,
of how, when Giordano
climbed to his burning
he could not find
in any human tongue
words for mankind,
mankind who live on.

Already they were back at their wine
or peddled their white starfish,
baskets of olives and lemons
they had shouldered to the fair,
and he already distanced
as if centuries had passed
while they paused just a moment
for his flying in the fire.

Those dying here, the lonely
forgotten by the world,
our tongue becomes for them
the language of an ancient planet.

Until, when all is legend
and many years have passed,
on a new Campo dei Fiori
rage will kindle at a poet's word.

Warsaw, 1943

SONG OF A CITIZEN

A stone from the depths that has witnessed the seas drying up
and a million white fish leaping in agony,
I, poor man, see a multitude of white-bellied nations
without freedom. I see the crab feeding on their flesh.

I have seen the fall of States and the perdition of tribes,
the flight of kings and emperors, the power of tyrants.
I can say now, in this hour,
that I—am, while everything expires,
that it is better to be a live dog than a dead lion,
as the Scripture says.

A poor man, sitting on a cold chair, pressing my eyelids,
I sigh and think of a starry sky,
of non-Euclidean space, of amoebas and their pseudopodia,
of tall mounds of termites.

When walking, I am asleep, when sleeping, I dream reality,
pursued and covered with sweat, I run.
On city squares lifted up by the glaring dawn,
beneath marble remnants of blasted-down gates,
I deal in vodka and gold.

And yet so often I was near,
I reached into the heart of metal, the soul of earth, of fire, of water.
And the unknown unveiled its face
as a night reveals itself, serene, mirrored by tide.
Lustrous copper-leaved gardens greeted me
that disappear as soon as you touch them.

And so near, just outside the window—the greenhouse of the worlds
where a tiny beetle and a spider are equal to planets,
where a wandering atom flares up like Saturn,

and, close by, harvesters drink from a cold jug
in scorching summer.

This I wanted and nothing more. In my later years
like old Goethe to stand before the face of the earth,
and recognize it and reconcile it
with my work built up, a forest citadel
on a river of shifting lights and brief shadows.

This I wanted and nothing more. So who
is guilty? Who deprived me
of my youth and my ripe years, who seasoned
my best years with horror? Who,
who ever is to blame, who, O God?

And I can think only about the starry sky,
about the tall mounds of termites.

Warsaw, 1943

A POOR CHRISTIAN LOOKS
AT THE GHETTO

Bees build around red liver,
Ants build around black bone.
It has begun: the tearing, the trampling on silks,
It has begun: the breaking of glass, wood, copper, nickel, silver, foam
Of gypsum, iron sheets, violin strings, trumpets, leaves, balls, crystals.
Poof! Phosphorescent fire from yellow walls
Engulfs animal and human hair.

Bees build around the honeycomb of lungs,
Ants build around white bone.
Torn is paper, rubber, linen, leather, flax,
Fiber, fabrics, cellulose, snakeskin, wire.
The roof and the wall collapse in flame and heat seizes the foundations.
Now there is only the earth, sandy, trodden down,
With one leafless tree.

Slowly, boring a tunnel, a guardian mole makes his way,
With a small red lamp fastened to his forehead.
He touches buried bodies, counts them, pushes on,
He distinguishes human ashes by their luminous vapor,
The ashes of each man by a different part of the spectrum.
Bees build around a red trace.
Ants build around the place left by my body.

I am afraid, so afraid of the guardian mole.
He has swollen eyelids, like a Patriarch
Who has sat much in the light of candles
Reading the great book of the species.

What will I tell him, I, a Jew of the New Testament,
Waiting two thousand years for the second coming of Jesus?
My broken body will deliver me to his sight
And he will count me among the helpers of death:
The uncircumcised.

Warsaw, 1943

THE WORLD

The Road

There where you see a green valley
And a road half-covered with grass,
Through an oak wood beginning to bloom
Children are returning home from school.

In a pencil case that opens sideways
Crayons rattle among crumbs of a roll
And a copper penny saved by every child
To greet the first spring cuckoo.

Sister's beret and brother's cap
Bob in the bushy underbrush,
A screeching jay hops in the branches
And long clouds float over the trees.

A red roof is already visible at the bend.
In front of the house father, leaning on a hoe,
Bows down, touches the unfolded leaves,
And from his flower bed inspects the whole region.

The Gate

Later dense hops will cover it completely.
As for now, it has the color
That lily pads have in very deep water
When you pluck them in the light of a summer evening.

The pickets are painted white at the top.
White and sharp, like tiny flames.
Strange that this never bothered the birds.
Even a wild pigeon once perched there.

The handle is of wood worn smooth over time,
Polished by the touch of many hands.
Nettles like to steal under the handle
And a yellow jasmine here is a tiny lantern.

The Porch

The porch whose doors face the west
Has large windows. The sun warms it well.
From here you can see north, south, east, and west,
Forests and rivers, fields and tree-lined lanes.

When the oaks array themselves in green
And the linden's shade reaches the flower bed,
The world disappears behind the blue bark,
Engraved by leaves into motley patches.

Here, at a tiny table, brother and sister
Kneel, drawing scenes of battle and pursuit.
And with their pink tongues try to help
Great warships, one of which is sinking.

The Dining Room

A room with low windows, with brown shades,
Where a Danzig clock keeps silent in the corner;
A low leather sofa; and right above it
The sculpted heads of two smiling devils;
And a copper pan shows its gleaming paunch.

On the wall a painting that depicts winter.
A crowd of people skate on ice

Between the trees, smoke comes from a chimney,
And crows fly in an overcast sky.

Nearby a second clock. A bird sits inside.
It pops out squawking and calls three times.
And it has barely finished its third and last call
When mother ladles out soup from a hot tureen.

The Stairs

Yellow, creaking, and smelling of wax
The curved steps are narrow. Near the wall
You can place your shoe crosswise
But near the banister they hardly hold your foot.

The boar's head is alive, enormous in shadow.
At first, just the tusks, then as it grows
The snout roams the ceiling, sniffing the stairway vault
While the light dissolves into vibrating dust.

Mother carries down a flickering light.
She walks slowly, tall, her robe tied at the waist,
Her shadow climbs up to the shadow of the boar.
And so she struggles, alone, with the cruel beast.

Pictures

The book is open. A moth with its shaky flight
Flits over a chariot that speeds through the dust.
Touched, it falls down pouring a golden spray
On a Greek army storming a city.

Behind a speeding chariot they drag the hero.
His head bumps against stone slabs.
While the moth, pinned to the page by the slap of a hand,
Flutters and dies on the hero's body.

And here, the sky gets cloudy, thunder resounds,
Ships clear the rocks for the open sea.
On the shore oxen lower their yoked necks
And a naked man ploughs the field.

Father in the Library

A high forehead, and above it tousled hair
On which a ray of sun falls from the window.
And so father wears a bright fluffy crown
When he spreads before him a huge book.

His gown is patterned like that of a wizard.
Softly, he murmurs his incantations.
Only he whom God instructs in magic
Will learn what wonders are hidden in this book.

Father's Incantations

O sweet master, with how much peace
Your serene wisdom fills the heart!
I love you, I am in your power
Even though I will never see your face.

Your ashes have long been scattered,
Your sins and follies no one remembers.
And for ages you will remain perfect
Like your book drawn by thought from nothingness.

You knew bitterness and you knew doubt
But the memory of your faults has vanished.
And I know why I cherish you today:
Men are small but their works are great.

From the Window

Beyond a field, a wood and a second field,
The expanse of water, a white mirror, glitters.
And the golden lowland of the earth
Bathes in the sea, a half-sunken tulip.

Father tells us that this is Europe.
On sunny days you can see it all clearly.
Now it is smoking after many floods,
A home for people, dogs, cats, and horses.

The bright towers of cities shine there,
Streams intertwine their silver threads,
And the moons of mountains are visible in spots,
Something like goose feathers scattered on the ground.

Father Explains

"There where that ray touches the plain
And the shadows escape as if they really ran,
Warsaw stands, open from all sides,
A city not very old but quite famous.

"Farther, where strings of rain hang from a little cloud,
Under the hills with an acacia grove
Is Prague. Above it, a marvelous castle
Shored against a slope in accordance with old rules.

"What divides this land with white foam
Is the Alps. The black means fir forests.
Beyond them, bathing in the yellow sun
Italy lies, like a deep-blue dish.

"Among the many fine cities that are there
You will recognize Rome, Christendom's capital,
By those round roofs on the church
Called the Basilica of Saint Peter.

"And there, to the north, beyond a bay,
Where a level bluish mist moves in waves,
Paris tries to keep pace with its tower
And reins in its herd of bridges.

"Also other cities accompany Paris,
They are adorned with glass, arrayed in iron,
But for today that would be too much,
I'll tell the rest another time."

A Parable of the Poppy

On a poppy seed is a tiny house,
Dogs bark at the poppy-seed moon,
And never, never do those poppy-seed dogs
Imagine that somewhere there is a world much larger.

The Earth is a seed—and really no more,
While other seeds are planets and stars.
And even if there were a hundred thousand,
Each might have a house and a garden.

All in a poppy head. The poppy grows tall,
The children run by and the poppy sways.
And in the evening, under the rising moon,
Dogs bark somewhere, now loudly, now softly.

By the Peonies

The peonies bloom, white and pink.
And inside each, as in a fragrant bowl,
A swarm of tiny beetles have their conversation,
For the flower is given to them as their home.

Mother stands by the peony bed,
Reaches for one bloom, opens its petals,
And looks for a long time into peony lands,
Where one short instant equals a whole year.

Then lets the flower go. And what she thinks
She repeats aloud to the children and herself.
The wind sways the green leaves gently
And speckles of light flick across their faces.

Faith

Faith is in you whenever you look
At a dewdrop or a floating leaf
And know that they are because they have to be.
Even if you close your eyes and dream up things
The world will remain as it has always been
And the leaf will be carried by the waters of the river.

You have faith also when you hurt your foot
Against a sharp rock and you know

That rocks are here to hurt our feet.
See the long shadow that is cast by the tree?
We and the flowers throw shadows on the earth.
What has no shadow has no strength to live.

Hope

Hope is with you when you believe
The earth is not a dream but living flesh,
That sight, touch, and hearing do not lie,
That all things you have ever seen here
Are like a garden looked at from a gate.

You cannot enter. But you're sure it's there.
Could we but look more clearly and wisely
We might discover somewhere in the garden
A strange new flower and an unnamed star.

Some people say we should not trust our eyes,
That there is nothing, just a seeming,
These are the ones who have no hope.
They think that the moment we turn away,
The world, behind our backs, ceases to exist,
As if snatched up by the hands of thieves.

Love

Love means to learn to look at yourself
The way one looks at distant things
For you are only one thing among many.
And whoever sees that way heals his heart,

Without knowing it, from various ills—
A bird and a tree say to him: Friend.

Then he wants to use himself and things
So that they stand in the glow of ripeness.
It doesn't matter whether he knows what he serves:
Who serves best doesn't always understand.

The Excursion to the Forest

The trees so huge you can't see treetops.
The setting sun fixes a rosy flame
On every tree, as on a candlestick,
And tiny people walk a path below.

Let us raise our heads, hold hands
So that we don't lose our way in the tangled grass.
The night has begun to put seals on the flowers,
Color after color is flowing down the sky.

And there, above, a feast. Jugs of gold,
Red wine is being poured in aspen copper.
And an airborne coach carries gifts
For the invisible kings or for the bears.

The Bird Kingdom

Flying high the heavy wood grouse
Slash the forest sky with their wings
And a pigeon returns to its airy wilderness
And a raven gleams with airplane steel.

What is the earth for them? A lake of darkness.
It has been swallowed by the night forever.
They, above the dark as above black waves,
Have their homes and islands, saved by the light.

If they groom their long feathers with their beaks
And drop one of them, it floats a long time
Before it reaches the bottom of the lake
And brushes someone's face, bringing news
From a world that is bright, beautiful, warm, and free.

Fear

"Father, where are you? The forest is wild,
There are creatures here, the bushes sway.
The orchids burst with poisonous fire,
Treacherous chasms lurk under our feet.

"Where are you, Father? The night has no end.
From now on darkness will last forever.
The travelers are homeless, they will die of hunger,
Our bread is bitter and hard as stone.

"The hot breath of the terrible beast
Comes nearer and nearer, it belches its stench.
Where have you gone, Father? Why do you not pity
Your children lost in this murky wood?"

Recovery

"Here I am—why this senseless fear?
The night is over, the day will soon arise.

You hear? The shepherds' horns already sound,
And stars grow pale over the rosy glow.

"The path is straight. We are at the edge.
Down in the village the little bell chimes.
Roosters on the fences greet the light
And the earth steams, fertile and happy.

"Here it is still dark. Fog like a river flood
Swaddles the black clumps of bilberries.
But the dawn on bright stilts wades in from the shore
And the ball of the sun, ringing, rolls."

The Sun

All colors come from the sun. And it does not have
Any particular color, for it contains them all.
And the whole Earth is like a poem
While the sun above represents the artist.

Whoever wants to paint the variegated world
Let him never look straight up at the sun
Or he will lose the memory of things he has seen.
Only burning tears will stay in his eyes.

Let him kneel down, lower his face to the grass,
And look at light reflected by the ground.
There he will find everything we have lost:
The stars and the roses, the dusks and the dawns.

Warsaw, 1943

A SONG ON THE END
OF THE WORLD

On the day the world ends
A bee circles a clover,
A fisherman mends a glimmering net.
Happy porpoises jump in the sea,
By the rainspout young sparrows are playing
And the snake is gold-skinned as it should always be.

On the day the world ends
Women walk through the fields under their umbrellas,
A drunkard grows sleepy at the edge of a lawn,
Vegetable peddlers shout in the street
And a yellow-sailed boat comes nearer the island,
The voice of a violin lasts in the air
And leads into a starry night.

And those who expected lightning and thunder
Are disappointed.
And those who expected signs and archangels' trumps
Do not believe it is happening now.
As long as the sun and the moon are above,
As long as the bumblebee visits a rose,
As long as rosy infants are born
No one believes it is happening now.

Only a white-haired old man, who would be a prophet
Yet is not a prophet, for he's much too busy,
Repeats while he binds his tomatoes:
No other end of the world will there be,
No other end of the world will there be.

Warsaw, 1944

CAFÉ

Of those at the table in the café
where on winter noons a garden of frost glittered on windowpanes
I alone survived.
I could go in there if I wanted to
and drumming my fingers in a chilly void
convoke shadows.

With disbelief I touch the cold marble,
with disbelief I touch my own hand.
It—is, and I—am in ever novel becoming,
while they are locked forever and ever
in their last word, their last glance,
and as remote as Emperor Valentinian
or the chiefs of the Massagetes, about whom I know nothing,
though hardly one year has passed, or two or three.

I may still cut trees in the woods of the far north,
I may speak from a platform or shoot a film
using techniques they never heard of.
I may learn the taste of fruits from ocean islands
and be photographed in attire from the second half of the century.
But they are forever like busts in frock coats and jabots
in some monstrous encyclopedia.

Sometimes when the evening aurora paints the roofs in a poor street
and I contemplate the sky, I see in the white clouds
a table wobbling. The waiter whirls with his tray
and they look at me with a burst of laughter
for I still don't know what it is to die at the hand of man,
they know—they know it well.

Warsaw, 1944

OUTSKIRTS

A hand with cards drops down
on the hot sand.
The sun turned white drops down
on the hot sand.
Ted holds the bank. Now Ted is dealing.
The glare stabs through the sticky pack
into hot sand.

A broken shadow of a chimney. Thin grass.
Farther on, the city torn into red brick.
Brown heaps, barbed wire tangled at stations.
Dry rib of a rusty automobile.
A claypit glitters.

An empty bottle buried
in the hot sand.
A drop of rain raised dust
off the hot sand.
Frank holds the bank. Now Frank is dealing.
We play, Julys and Mays go by.
We play one year, we play a fourth.
The glare pours through our blackened cards
into hot sand.

Farther on, the city torn into red brick.
A lone pine tree behind a Jewish house.
Loose footprints and the plain up to the horizon.
The dust of quicklime, wagons rolling,
and in the wagons a whining lament.

Take a mandolin, on the mandolin
you'll play it all.
Heigh-ho. Fingers, strings.
So nice a song.

A barren field.
The glass tossed off.
No more is needed.

Look, there she goes, a pretty girl.
Cork-soled slippers and curly hair.
Hello sweetheart, let's have a good time.
A barren field.
The sun is setting.

Warsaw, 1944

FLIGHT

When we were fleeing the burning city
And looked back from the first field path,
I said: "Let the grass grow over our footprints,
Let the harsh prophets fall silent in the fire,
Let the dead explain to the dead what happened.
We are fated to beget a new and violent tribe
Free from the evil and the happiness that drowsed there.
Let us go"—and the earth was opened for us by a sword of flames.

Goszyce, 1944

from A TREATISE ON POETRY

...

III. THE SPIRIT OF HISTORY

Under a linden tree, as before, daylight
Quivered on a goose quill dipped in ink.
Books were still governed by the old rule,
Born of a belief that visible beauty
Is a little mirror for the beauty of being.
The survivors ran through fields, escaping
From themselves, knowing they wouldn't return
For a hundred years. Before them were spread
Those quicksands where a tree changes into nothing,
Into an anti-tree, where no borderline
Separates a shape from a shape, and where,
Amid thunder, the golden house of *is*
Collapses, and the word *becoming* ascends.

Till the end of their days all of them
Carried the memory of their cowardice,
For they didn't want to die without a reason.
Now He, expected, for a long time awaited,
Raised up the smoke of a thousand censers.
They crawled on slippery paths to his feet.

—"King of the centuries, ungraspable Movement,
You who fill the gotttoes of the ocean
With a rolling silence, who dwell in the blood
Of the gored shark devoured by other sharks,
In the whistle of a half-bird, half-fish,
In the thundering sea, in the iron gurgling
Of the rocks when archipelagoes surge up.

"The churning of your surf casts up bracelets,
Pearls not eyes, bones from which the salt
Has eaten crowns and dresses of brocade.
You without beginning, you always between

A form and a form, O stream, bright spark,
Antithesis that ripens toward a thesis,
Now we have become equal to the gods,
Knowing, in you, that we do not exist.

"You, in whom cause is married to effect,
Drew us from the depth as you draw a wave,
For one instant, limitless, of transformation.
You have shown us the agony of this age
So that we could ascend to those heights
Where your hand commands the instruments.
Spare us, do not punish us. Our offense
Was grave: we forgot the power of your law.
Save us from ignorance. Accept now our devotion."

So they forswore. But every one of them
Kept hidden a hope that the possessions of time
Were assigned a limit. That they would one day
Be able to look at a cherry tree in blossom,
For a moment, unique among the moments,
Put the ocean to sleep, close the hourglass,
And listen to how the clocks stop ticking.

When they put a rope around my neck,
When they choke off my breath with a rope,
I'll turn around once, and what will I be?

When they give me an injection of phenol,
When I walk half a step with phenol in my veins,
What wisdom of the prophets will enlighten me?

When they tear us from this one embrace,
When they destroy forever the shaft of tender light,
What Heaven will see us reunited?

Warsaw, 1939–1945

IN WARSAW

What are you doing here, poet, on the ruins
Of St. John's Cathedral this sunny
Day in spring?

What are you thinking here, where the wind
Blowing from the Vistula scatters
The red dust of the rubble?

You swore never to be
A ritual mourner.
You swore never to touch
The deep wounds of your nation
So you would not make them holy
With the accursed holiness that pursues
Descendants for many centuries.

But the lament of Antigone
Searching for her brother
Is indeed beyond the power
Of endurance. And the heart
Is a stone in which is enclosed,
Like an insect, the dark love
Of a most unhappy land.

I did not want to love so.
That was not my design.
I did not want to pity so.
That was not my design.
My pen is lighter
Than a hummingbird's feather. This burden
Is too much for it to bear.
How can I live in this country
Where the foot knocks against
The unburied bones of kin?

I hear voices, see smiles. I cannot
Write anything; five hands
Seize my pen and order me to write
The story of their lives and deaths.
Was I born to become
a ritual mourner?
I want to sing of festivities,
The greenwood into which Shakespeare
Often took me. Leave
To poets a moment of happiness,
Otherwise your world will perish.

It's madness to live without joy
And to repeat to the dead
Whose part was to be gladness
Of action in thought and in the flesh, singing, feasts,
Only the two salvaged words:
Truth and justice.

Warsaw, 1945

DEDICATION

You whom I could not save
Listen to me.
Try to understand this simple speech as I would be ashamed of another.
I swear, there is in me no wizardry of words.
I speak to you with silence like a cloud or a tree.

What strengthened me, for you was lethal.
You mixed up farewell to an epoch with the beginning of a new one,
Inspiration of hatred with lyrical beauty,
Blind force with accomplished shape.

Here is a valley of shallow Polish rivers. And an immense bridge
Going into white fog. Here is a broken city,
And the wind throws the screams of gulls on your grave
When I am talking with you.

What is poetry which does not save
Nations or people?
A connivance with official lies,
A song of drunkards whose throats will be cut in a moment,
Readings for sophomore girls.

That I wanted good poetry without knowing it,
That I discovered, late, its salutary aim,
In this and only this I find salvation.

They used to pour millet on graves or poppy seeds
To feed the dead who would come disguised as birds.
I put this book here for you, who once lived
So that you should visit us no more.

Warsaw, 1945

MID-TWENTIETH-CENTURY
PORTRAIT

Hidden behind his smile of brotherly regard,
He despises the newspaper reader, the victim of the dialectic of power.
Says: "Democracy," with a wink.
Hates the physiological pleasures of mankind,
Full of memories of those who also ate, drank, copulated,
But in a moment had their throats cut.
Recommends dances and garden parties to defuse public anger.

Shouts: "Culture!" and "Art!" but means circus games really.

Utterly spent.
Mumbles in sleep or anaesthesia: "God, oh God!"
Compares himself to a Roman in whom the Mithras cult has mixed
    with the cult of Jesus.
Still clings to old superstitions, sometimes believes himself to be
    possessed by demons.
Attacks the past, but fears that, having destroyed it,
He will have nothing on which to lay his head.
Likes most to play cards, or chess, the better to keep his own counsel.

Keeping one hand on Marx's writings, he reads the Bible in private.
His mocking eye on processions leaving burned-out churches.
His backdrop: a horseflesh-colored city in ruins.
In his hand: a memento of a boy "fascist" killed in the Uprising.

Kraków, 1945

SONG ON PORCELAIN

Rose-colored cup and saucer,
Flowery demitasses:
You lie beside the river
Where an armored column passes.
Winds from across the meadow
Sprinkle the banks with down;
A torn apple tree's shadow
Falls on the muddy path;
The ground everywhere is strewn
With bits of brittle froth—
Of all things broken and lost
Porcelain troubles me most.

Before the first red tones
Begin to warm the sky
The earth wakes up, and moans.
It is the small sad cry
Of cups and saucers cracking,
The masters' precious dream
Of roses, of mowers raking,
And shepherds on the lawn.
The black underground stream
Swallows the frozen swan.
This morning, as I walked past,
The porcelain troubled me most.

The blackened plain spreads out
To where the horizon blurs
In a litter of handle and spout,
A lively pulp that stirs
And crunches under my feet.
Pretty, useless foam:
Your stained colors are sweet,
Spattered in dirty waves

Flecking the fresh black loam
In the mounds of these new graves.
In sorrow and pain and cost,
Sir, porcelain troubles me most.

Washington, D.C., 1947

GREEK PORTRAIT

My beard is thick, my eyelids half cover
My eyes, as with those who know the value
Of visible things. I keep quiet as is proper
For a man who has learned that the human heart
Holds more than speech does. I have left behind
My native land, home, and public office.
Not that I looked for profit or adventure.
I am no foreigner on board a ship.
My plain face, the face of a tax-collector,
Merchant, or soldier, makes me one of the crowd.
Nor do I refuse to pay due homage
To local gods. And I eat what others eat.
About myself, this much will suffice.

Washington, D.C., 1948

EARTH

My sweet European homeland,

A butterfly lighting on your flowers stains its wings with blood,
Blood gathers in the mouths of tulips,
Shines, star-like, inside a morning glory
And washes the grains of wheat.

Your people warm their hands
At the funeral candle of a primrose
And hear on the fields the wind howling
In the cannons ready to be fired.

You are a land where it's no shame to suffer
For one is served here a glass of bitter liquor
With lees, the poison of centuries.

On your broken evening of wet leaves,
By the waters that carry the rust
Of centurions' sunken armor,
At the foot of blasted towers,
In the shadow of their spans like aqueducts,
Under the quiet canopy of an owl's wings,

A red poppy, touched by the ice of tears.

Washington, D.C., 1949

MITTELBERGHEIM

Wine sleeps in casks of Rhine oak.
I am wakened by the bell of a chapel in the vineyards
Of Mittelbergheim. I hear a small spring
Trickling into a well in the yard, a clatter
Of sabots in the street. Tobacco drying
Under the eaves, and ploughs and wooden wheels
And mountain slopes and autumn are with me.

I keep my eyes closed. Do not rush me,
You, fire, power, might, for it is too early.
I have lived through many years and, as in this half-dream,
I felt I was attaining the moving frontier
Beyond which color and sound come true
And the things of this earth are united.
Do not yet force me to open my lips.
Let me trust and believe I will attain.
Let me linger here in Mittelbergheim.

I know I should. They are with me,
Autumn and wooden wheels and tobacco hung
Under the eaves. Here and everywhere
Is my homeland, wherever I turn
And in whatever language I would hear
The song of a child, the conversation of lovers.
Happier than anyone, I am to receive
A glance, a smile, a star, silk creased
At the knee. Serene, beholding,
I am to walk on hills in the soft glow of day
Over waters, cities, roads, human customs.

Fire, power, might, you who hold me
In the palm of your hand whose furrows
Are like immense gorges combed

By southern wind. You who grant certainty
In the hour of fear, in the week of doubt,
It is too early, let the wine mature,
Let the travelers sleep in Mittelbergheim.

Alsace, 1951

ESSE

I looked at that face, dumbfounded. The lights of *métro* stations flew by; I didn't notice them. What can be done, if our sight lacks absolute power to devour objects ecstatically, in an instant, leaving nothing more than the void of an ideal form, a sign like a hieroglyph simplified from the drawing of an animal or bird? A slightly snub nose, a high brow with sleekly brushed-back hair, the line of the chin—but why isn't the power of sight absolute?—and in a whiteness tinged with pink two sculpted holes, containing a dark, lustrous lava. To absorb that face but to have it simultaneously against the background of all spring boughs, walls, waves, in its weeping, its laughter, moving it back fifteen years, or ahead thirty. To have. It is not even a desire. Like a butterfly, a fish, the stem of a plant, only more mysterious. And so it befell me that after so many attempts at naming the world, I am able only to repeat, harping on one string, the highest, the unique avowal beyond which no power can attain: *I am, she is.* Shout, blow the trumpets, make thousands-strong marches, leap, rend your clothing, repeating only: *is!*

She got out at Raspail. I was left behind with the immensity of existing things. A sponge, suffering because it cannot saturate itself; a river, suffering because reflections of clouds and trees are not clouds and trees.

Brie-Comte-Robert, 1954

ALBUM OF DREAMS

May 10
Did I mistake the house or the street
or perhaps the staircase, though once I was there every day?
I looked through the keyhole. The kitchen: the same and not the same.
And I carried, wound on a reel,
a plastic tape, narrow as a shoelace,
that was everything I had written over the long years.
I rang, uncertain whether I would hear that name.
She stood before me in her saffron dress,
unchanged, greeting me with a smile without one tear of time.
And in the morning chickadees were singing in the cedar.

June 17
And that snow will remain forever,
unredeemed, not spoken of to anyone.
On it their track freezes at sunset
in an hour, in a year, in a district, in a country.

And that face will remain forever
beaten for ages by drops of rain.
One drop is running from eyelid to lip
on an empty square, in an unnamed city.

August 14
They ordered us to pack our things, as the house was to be burned.
There was time to write a letter, but that letter was with me.
We laid down our bundles and sat against the wall.
They looked when we placed a violin on the bundles.
My little sons did not cry. Gravity and curiosity.
One of the soldiers brought a can of gasoline. Others were tearing
        down curtains.

November 18
He showed us a road which led down.
We would not get lost, he said, there were many lights.
Through abandoned orchards, vineyards and embankments
overgrown with brambles we took a shortcut,
and the lights were, as you will—the lanterns
of gigantic glowworms, or small planets
descending in uncertain flight.
Once, when we tried to make a turn up
everything went out. And in total darkness
I understood we must march on into the gorge
since only then the lights would lead us again.
I held her hand, we were united
by bodily memory
of journeying together on a lovers' bed,
that is to say, one time in the wheat or a dense forest.
Below a torrent roared, there were frozen rockslides
the atrocious color of lunar sulphur.

November 23
A long train is standing in the station and the platform is empty.
Winter, night, the frozen sky is flooded with red.
Only a woman's weeping is heard. She is pleading for something
from an officer in a stone coat.

December 1
The halls of the infernal station, drafty and cold.
A knock at the door, the door opens
and my dead father appears in the doorway
but he is young, handsome, beloved.
He offers me his hand. I run away from him
down a spiral staircase, never-ending.

December 3
With a broad white beard and dressed in velvet,
Walt Whitman was leading dances in a country manor
owned by Swedenborg, Emanuel.
And I was there as well, drinking mead and wine.
At first we circled hand in hand
and resembled stones overgrown with mold,
set into motion. Then the invisible
orchestras played more quickly, and we were seized
by the madness of the dance, in elation.
And that dance, of harmony, of concord
was a dance of happy Hassidim.

December 14
I moved my strong wings, below were gliding
bluish meadows, willows, a winding river.
Here is the castle with its moat, and nearby, the gardens
where my beloved takes a walk.
But as I returned, I had to take care
not to lose the magic book
stuck in my belt. I could never manage
to soar very high, and there were mountains.
I struggled painfully to the ridge above the forest
rusty from the leaves of oaks and chestnuts.
There, at birds carved on a dry branch,
an invisible hand was throwing boughs
to draw me down by magic means.
I fell. She kept me on her glove,
now a hawk with bloodstained plume,
the Witch of the Desert. In the castle she had found out
the incantations printed in my book.

March 16

The unsummoned face. How he died no one knows.
I repeated my question until he took flesh.
And he, a boxer, hits the guard in the jaw,
for which boots trample him. I look at the guard
with dog's eyes and have one desire:
to carry out every order, so he will praise me.
And even when he sent me to the city,
a city of arcades, of passages, of marble squares
(it seems to be Venice), stepping on the slabs,
in funny rags, barefoot, with an oversize cap,
I think of fulfilling only what he assigned me,
I show my permits and carry for him
a Japanese doll (the vendor didn't know its value).

March 24

It is a country on the edge of the Rudnicka Wilderness,
for example, beside the sawmill at Jashuny, between the fir-forest of
     Kiejdzie
and the villages of Czernica, Mariampol, Halina.
Perhaps the river Yerres runs there
between banks of anemones on marshy meadows.
The inseminator-pines, footbridges, tall ferns.
How the earth heaves! Not in order to burst,
but it tells with a movement of its skin
that it can make trees bow to one another and tumble down.
For that reason joy. Such as people never
have known before. Rejoice! Rejoice!
in a path, in a shack, in a protruding stone.
And water! But in that water whatever you shoot sinks.
Joseph, smelling of cheap tobacco, stands on the bank.
—I shot a bear, but it fell in.—When?

—This afternoon.—Stupid, look, see that keg?
There's your bear, floating in it. Where's the bear? Shame.
It's only a wounded bear cub breathing.

March 26
Through the meadow fields at night,
through the meadow fields of civilization
we ran shouting, singing, in a tongue not our own
but one which terrified others.
They ran before us, we took two-yard,
three-yard strides,
limitlessly powerful, happy.
Turning out its lights, a car stopped: a different one,
a car from there. We heard voices
speaking near us in a tongue we had used only for amusement.
Now we, the pretenders, were seized by fear
so great that over fences and palisades
in fourteen-yard leaps we ran into the depths of the forest.
And behind us the hue and cry
in a Scythian or Lombard dialect.

April 3
Our expedition rode into a land of dry lava.
Perhaps under us were armor and crowns
but here there was not a tree,
or even lichens growing on the rocks,
and in the birdless sky, racing through filmy clouds
the sun went down between black concretions.

When slowly, in that complete stillness
in which not a lizard was rustling
gravel began to crunch under the wheels of the trucks

suddenly we saw, standing on a hill,
a pink corset with ribbon floating.
Further a second and a third. So, baring our heads,
we walked toward them, temples in ruins.

Montgeron, 1955

NO MORE

I should relate sometime how I changed
My views on poetry, and how it came to be
That I consider myself today one of the many
Merchants and artisans of Old Japan,
Who arranged verses about cherry blossoms,
Chrysanthemums and the full moon.

If only I could describe the courtesans of Venice
As in a loggia they teased a peacock with a twig,
And out of brocade, the pearls of their belt,
Set free heavy breasts and the reddish weal
Where the buttoned dress marked the belly,
As vividly as seen by the skipper of galleons
Who landed that morning with a cargo of gold;
And if I could find for their miserable bones
In a graveyard whose gates are licked by greasy water
A word more enduring than their last-used comb
That in the rot under tombstones, alone, awaits the light,

Then I wouldn't doubt. Out of reluctant matter
What can be gathered? Nothing, beauty at best.
And so, cherry blossoms must suffice for us
And chrysanthemums and the full moon.

Montgeron, 1957

MAGPIETY

The same and not quite the same, I walked through oak forests
Amazed that my Muse, Mnemosyne,
Has in no way diminished my amazement.
A magpie was screeching and I said: Magpiety?
What is magpiety? I shall never achieve
A magpie heart, a hairy nostril over the beak, a flight
That always renews just when coming down,
And so I shall never comprehend magpiety.
If however magpiety does not exist
My nature does not exist either.
Who would have guessed that, centuries later,
I would invent the question of universals?

Montgeron, 1958

THROUGHOUT OUR LANDS

1

When I pass'd through a populous city
(as Walt Whitman says, in the Polish version)
When I pass'd through a populous city,
for instance near San Francisco harbor, counting gulls,
I thought that between men, women, and children there is
something, neither happiness nor unhappiness.

2

At noon white rubble of cemeteries on the hillsides:
a city of eye-dazzling cements
glued together with the slime of winged insects
spins with the sky about the spiraled freeways.

3

If I had to tell what the world is for me
I would take a hamster or a hedgehog or a mole
and place him in a theater seat one evening
and, bringing my ear close to his humid snout,
would listen to what he says about the spotlights,
sounds of the music, and movements of the dance.

4

Was I breaking the sound barrier?
And then clouds with cathedrals,
ecstatic greens beyond wrought-iron gates
and silence, surprisingly, different from what I'd known.
Here I am where the fist of an old woman is wrapped with a rosary,
a cane taps on flagstones between dappled shadows.
Is it a shame or not
that this is my portion?

5

Waking before dawn, I saw the gray lake
and, as usual, two men trolling in a motorboat, which sputtered slowly.
Next, I was awakened by the sun shining straight into my eyes
as it stood above the pass on the Nevada side.
Between the moment and the moment I lived through much in my
    sleep
so distinctly that I felt time dissolve
and knew that what was past still is, not was.
And I hope this will be counted somehow in my defense:
my regret and great longing once to express
one life, not for my glory, for a different splendor.
Later on a slight wind creased the iridescent water.
I was forgetting. Snow glittered on the mountains.

6

And the word revealed out of darkness was: pear.
I hovered around it hopping or trying my wings.
But whenever I was just about to drink its sweetness, it withdrew.
So I tried Anjou—then a garden's corner,
scaling white paint of wooden shutters,
a dogwood bush and rustling of departed people.
So I tried Comice—then right away fields
beyond this (not another) palisade, a brook, countryside.
So I tried Jargonelle, Bosc, and Bergamot.
No good. Between me and pear, equipages, countries.
And so I have to live, with this spell on me.

7

With their chins high, girls come back from the tennis courts.
The spray rainbows over the sloping lawns.

With short jerks a robin runs up, stands motionless.
The eucalyptus tree trunks glow in the light.
The oaks perfect the shadow of May leaves.
Only this is worthy of praise. Only this: the day.

But beneath it elemental powers are turning somersaults;
and devils, mocking the naive who believe in them,
play catch with hunks of bloody meat,
whistle songs about matter without beginning or end,
and about the moment of our death
when everything we have cherished will appear
an artifice of cunning self-love.

8
And what if Pascal had not been saved
and if those narrow hands in which we laid a cross
are all he is, entire, like a lifeless swallow
in the dust, under the buzz of the poisonous-blue flies?

And if they all, kneeling with poised palms,
millions, billions of them, ended together with their illusion?
I shall never agree. I will give them the crown.
The human mind is splendid; lips powerful,
and the summons so great it must open Paradise.

9
They are so persistent, that give them a few stones
and edible roots, and they will build the world.

10
Over his grave they were playing Mozart,
Since they had nothing to keep themselves distinct

From the yellow dirt, clouds, wilted dahlias,
And under a sky too big, there was too much silence.

And just as at the tea party of a princess
When a stalactite of wax drips out the measure,
And a wick sizzles, and shoulders in frock coats
Gleam in their rows of high gold-braided collars,

Mozart has sounded, unwrapped from the powder of wigs,
And suspended on trails of late-summer gossamer,
Vanishing overhead, in that void where
A jet has gone, leaving a thin white seam.

While he, a contemporary of no one,
Black as a grub beneath the winter bark,
Was at work already, calling in rust and mold
So as to vanish, before they took the faded wreaths.

II

Paulina, her room behind the servants' quarters, with one window on
    the orchard
where I gather the best apples near the pigsty
squishing with my big toe the warm muck of the dunghill,
and the other window on the well (I love to drop the bucket down
and scare its inhabitants, the green frogs).
Paulina, a geranium, the chill of a dirt floor,
a hard bed with three pillows,
an iron crucifix and images of the saints,
decorated with palms and paper roses.
Paulina died long ago, but is.
And, I am somehow convinced, not just in my consciousness.
Above her rough Lithuanian peasant face
hovers a spindle of hummingbirds, and her flat calloused feet
are sprinkled by sapphire water in which dolphins
with their backs arching
frolic.

12
Wherever you are, colors of the sky envelop you
just as here, shrill oranges and violets,
the smell of a leaf pulped in your fingers accompanies you
even in your dream, birds are named
in the language of that place: a *towhee* came to the kitchen,
scatter some bread on the lawn, *juncos* have arrived.
Wherever you are, you touch the bark of trees
testing its roughness different yet familiar.
Grateful for a rising and a setting sun
Wherever you are, you could never be an alien.

Was Father Junipero an alien, when on mule-back
he came here, wandering through the deserts of the south.
He found redskin brothers. Their reason and memory
were dimmed. They had been roaming very far
from the Euphrates, the Pamirs, and the heights of Cathay,
slowly, as far as any generation can
pursuing its goal: good hunting grounds.
And there, where later the land sank into the cold
shallow sea, they had lived thousands of years,
until they had almost completely forgotten the Garden of Eden
and had not yet learned the reckoning of time.
Father Junipero, born on the Mediterranean,
brought them news about their first parents,
about the signs, the promise, and the expectation.
He told them, exiles, that there, in their native land,
their guilt had been washed away, just as dust is washed
from their foreheads, sprinkled with water.
It was like something they had heard of long ago.
But, poor people, they had lost the gift of concentration
and a preacher had to hang from his neck a roasted flank of deer
in order to attract their greedy eyes.
But then they slobbered, so loudly, he could not speak.

Nonetheless it was they who in my place took possession
of rocks on which only mute dragons
were basking from the beginning, crawling out of the sea.
They sewed a clock from the plumage of flickers, hummingbirds, and
    tanagers,
and a brown arm, throwing back the mantle, would point to: this.
And the land was henceforth conquered: seen.

13
Whiskers of rabbits and downy necks
of yellow-black ducklings, the flowing fire
of a fox in the green, touch the heart
of master and slave. And also musics
starting under the trees. A snare drum, a flute
or a concertina or from a gramophone
the voices of djinns bleating jazz.
A swing goes up to the clouds, and those looking from below
have their breath taken away by the darkness under a skirt.
Who has not dreamt of the Marquis de Sade's châteaux?
When one ("ah-h-h!") rubs his hands
and to the job: to gouge with a spur
young girls drawn up in line for footrace
or to order naked nuns in black net stockings
to lash us with a whip as we bite the bedsheets.

14
Cabeza, if anyone knew all about civilization, it was you.
A bookkeeper from Castile, what a fix you were in
to have to wander about, where no notion,
no cipher, no stroke of a pen dipped in sepia,
only a boat thrown up on the sand by surf,
crawling naked on all fours, under the eye of immobile Indians,
and suddenly their wail in the void of sky and sea,
their lament: that even the gods are unhappy.

For seven years you were their predicted god,
bearded, white-skinned, beaten if you couldn't work a miracle.
Seven years' march from the Mexican Gulf to California,
the hu-hu-hu of tribes, hot bramble of the continent.
But afterward? Who am I, the lace of cuffs
not mine, the table carved with lions not mine, Doña Clara's
fan, the slipper from under her gown—hell, no.
On all fours! On all fours!
Smear our thighs with war paint.
Lick the ground. Wha wha, hu hu.

Berkeley, 1961

VENI CREATOR

Come, Holy Spirit,
bending or not bending the grasses,
appearing or not above our heads in a tongue of flame,
at hay harvest or when they plough in the orchards or when snow
covers crippled firs in the Sierra Nevada.
I am only a man: I need visible signs.
I tire easily, building the stairway of abstraction.
Many a time I asked, you know it well, that the statue in church
lift its hand, only once, just once, for me.
But I understand that signs must be human,
therefore call one man, anywhere on earth,
not me—after all I have some decency—
and allow me, when I look at him, to marvel at you.

Berkeley, 1961

BOBO'S METAMORPHOSIS

The distance between being and nothingness is infinite.

—Entertainments Pleasant and Useful
(Zabawy przyjemne i pożyteczne, 1776)

I
Fields sloping down and a trumpet.

❦

Dusk and a bird flies low and waters flare.

❦

Sails unfurled to the daybreak beyond the straits.

❦

I was entering the interior of a lily by a bridge of brocade.

❦

Life was given but unattainable.

❦

From childhood till old age ecstasy at sunrise.

II
As life goes, many of these mornings.
My eyes closed, I was grown up and small.
I was wearing plumes, silks, ruffles and armor,
Women's dresses, I was licking the rouge.
I was hovering at each flower from the day of creation,
I knocked on the closed doors of the beaver's halls and the mole's.
It's incredible that there were so many unrecorded voices
Between a toothpaste and a rusted blade,
Just over my table in Wilno, Warsaw, Brie, Montgeron, California.
It's incredible that I die before I attain.

III
From the taste and scent of bird-cherry trees above rivers
Consciousness hikes through bay and hibiscus thickets

Gathering specimens of the Earth into a green box.
Above it, the red bark of *Sequoia sempervirens*
And jays, different from those beyond the Bering Strait,
Open their wings of indigo color.
Consciousness alone, without friends and foes,
Embraces forest slopes, an eagle's nest.
Incomprehensible as it is to a snake with a yellow stripe,
Itself unable to grasp the principle of the snake and tree.

IV
Stars of Philemon, stars of Baucis,
Above their house entangled by the roots of an oak.
And a wandering god, soundly asleep on a thong-strung bed,
His fist for a pillow.
An advancing weevil encounters his sandal
And pushes on painfully through a foot-polished mesa.

I hear also sounds of a pianoforte.
I steal through humid blackness under the jungle of spirea
Where are scattered clay flasks from Dutch aquavit.
She appears, a young lady with a curl on her ear.
But I grew a beard when walking on all fours
And my Indian bow rotted from snow and rain.
She plays music and simultaneously grows small, sits down on her
     chamberpot,
At a swing she pulls up her skirt
To do indecent things with me or her cousin.
And all of a sudden she walks grayhaired in a scraggy suburb,
Then departs without delay where all the maidens go.

Let there be an island—and an island crops out of the deep.
The pale rose of its cliffs is tinged with violet.
Seeds sprout, on the hills, presto, chestnuts and cedars,
A spring waves a fern just above the harbor.

On flat rocks over fir-green water of the cove
Spirits lounge, similar to skin divers with their oxygen tanks.
The only daughter of a sorcerer, Miranda,
Rides a donkey in the direction of the grotto
By a path strewn with creaking leaves.
She sees a tripod, a kettle, and bundles of dry twigs.
Vanish, island! Or stronger: go away!

V
I liked him as he did not look for an ideal object.
When he heard: "Only the object which does not exist
Is perfect and pure," he blushed and turned away.

In every pocket he carried pencils, pads of paper
Together with crumbs of bread, the accidents of life.

Year after year he circled a thick tree
Shading his eyes with his hand and muttering in amazement.

How much he envied those who draw a tree with one line!
But metaphor seemed to him something indecent.

He would leave symbols to the proud busy with their cause.
By looking he wanted to draw the name from the very thing.

When he was old, he tugged at his tobacco-stained beard:
"I prefer to lose thus than to win as they do."

Like Peter Breughel the father he fell suddenly
While attempting to look back between his spread-apart legs.

And still the tree stood there, unattainable.
Veritable, true to the very core.

VI

They reproached him with marrying one woman and living with
　　another.
Have no time—he answered—for nonsense, a divorce and so on.
A man gets up, a few strokes of a brush and then already it's evening.

VII

Bobo, a nasty boy, was changed into a fly.
In accordance with the rite of the flies he washed himself by a rock of
　　sugar
And ran vertically in caves of cheese.
He flew through a window into the bright garden.
There, indomitable ferryboats of leaves
Carried a drop taut with the excess of its rainbow,
Mossy parks grew by ponds of light in the mountains of bark,
An acrid dust was falling from flexible columns inside cinnabar flowers.
And though it did not last longer than from teatime till supper,
Later on, when he had pressed trousers and a trimmed moustache,
He always thought, holding a glass of liquor, that he was cheating them
For a fly should not discuss the nation and productivity.
A woman facing him was a volcanic peak
Where there were ravines, craters and in hollows of lava
The movement of earth was tilting crooked trunks of pines.

VIII

Between her and me there was a table, on the table a glass.
The chapped skin of her elbows touched the shining surface
In which the contour of shade under her armpit was reflected.
A drop of sweat thickened over her wavy lip.
And the space between her and me fractionized itself infinitely
Buzzing with pennate Eleatic arrows.
Not a year, not a hundred years of journey would exhaust it.
Had I overturned the table what would we have accomplished.

That act, a non-act, always no more than potential
Like the attempt to penetrate water, wood, minerals.
But she, too, looked at me as if I were a ring of Saturn
And knew I was aware that no one attains.
Thus were affirmed humanness, tenderness.

Berkeley, 1962

I SLEEP A LOT

I sleep a lot and read St. Thomas Aquinas
or *The Death of God* (that's a Protestant book).
To the right the bay as if molten tin,
beyond the bay, city, beyond the city, ocean,
beyond the ocean, ocean, till Japan.
To the left dry hills with white grass,
beyond the hills an irrigated valley where rice is grown,
beyond the valley, mountains and Ponderosa pines,
beyond the mountains, desert and sheep.

When I couldn't do without alcohol, I drove myself on alcohol,
When I couldn't do without cigarettes and coffee, I drove myself on
    cigarettes and coffee.
I was courageous. Industrious. Nearly a model of virtue.
But that is good for nothing.

Please, Doctor, I feel a pain.
Not here. No, not here. Even I don't know.
Maybe it's too many islands and continents,
unpronounced words, bazaars, wooden flutes,
or too much drinking to the mirror, without beauty,
though one was to be a kind of archangel
or a Saint George, over there, on St. George Street.

Please, Medicine Man, I feel a pain.
I always believed in spells and incantations.
Sure, women have only one, Catholic, soul,
but we have two. When you start to dance
you visit remote pueblos in your sleep
and even lands you have never seen.
Put on, I beg you, charms made of feathers,
now it's time to help one of your own.
I have read many books but I don't believe them.
When it hurts we return to the banks of certain rivers.

I remember those crosses with chiseled suns and moons
and wizards, how they worked during an outbreak of typhus.
Send your second soul beyond the mountains, beyond time.
Tell me what you saw, I will wait.

Berkeley, 1962

ELEGY FOR N. N.

Tell me if it is too far for you.
You could have run over the small waves of the Baltic
and past the fields of Denmark, past a beech wood
could have turned toward the ocean, and there, very soon
Labrador, white at this season.
And if you, who dreamed about a lonely island,
were frightened of cities and of lights flashing along the highway
you had a path straight through the wilderness
over blue-black, melting waters, with tracks of deer and caribou
as far as the Sierras and abandoned gold mines.
The Sacramento River could have led you
between hills overgrown with prickly oaks.
Then just a eucalyptus grove, and you had found me.

True, when the manzanita is in bloom
and the bay is clear on spring mornings
I think reluctantly of the house between the lakes
and of nets drawn in beneath the Lithuanian sky.
The bath cabin where you used to leave your dress
has changed forever into an abstract crystal.
Honey-like darkness is there, near the veranda,
and comic young owls, and the scent of leather.

How could one live at that time, I really can't say.
Styles and dresses flicker, indistinct,
not self-sufficient, tending toward a finale.
Does it matter that we long for things as they are in themselves?
The knowledge of fiery years has scorched the horses standing at the
    forge,
the little columns in the marketplace,
the wooden stairs and the wig of Mama Fliegeltaub.

We learned so much, this you know well:
how, gradually, what could not be taken away

is taken. People, countrysides.
And the heart does not die when one thinks it should,
we smile, there is tea and bread on the table.
And only remorse that we did not love
the poor ashes in Sachsenhausen
with absolute love, beyond human power.

You got used to new, wet winters,
to a villa where the blood of the German owner
was washed from the wall, and he never returned.
I too accepted but what was possible, cities and countries.
One cannot step twice into the same lake
on rotting alder leaves,
breaking a narrow sunstreak.

Guilt, yours and mine? Not a great guilt.
Secrets, yours and mine? Not great secrets.
Not when they bind the jaw with a kerchief, put a little cross between
      the fingers,
and somewhere a dog barks, and the first star flares up.

No, it was not because it was too far
you failed to visit me that day or night.
From year to year it grows in us until it takes hold,
I understood it as you did: indifference.

Berkeley, 1963

AND THE CITY STOOD
IN ITS BRIGHTNESS

And the city stood in its brightness when years later I returned.
And life was running out, Ruteboeuf's or Villon's.
Descendants, already born, were dancing their dances.
Women looked in their mirrors made from a new metal.
What was it all for if I cannot speak.
She stood above me, heavy, like the earth on its axis.
My ashes were laid in a can under the bistro counter.

And the city stood in its brightness when years later I returned
To my home in the display case of a granite museum,
Beside eyelash mascara, alabaster vials,
And menstruation girdles of an Egyptian princess.
There was only a sun forged out of gold plate,
On darkening parquetry the creak of unhurried steps.

And the city stood in its brightness when years later I returned,
My face covered with a coat though now no one was left
Of those who could have remembered my debts never paid,
My shames not forever, base deeds to be forgiven.
And the city stood in its brightness when years later I returned.

Paris—Berkeley, 1963

TO ROBINSON JEFFERS

If you have not read the Slavic poets
so much the better. There's nothing there
for a Scotch-Irish wanderer to seek. They lived in a childhood
prolonged from age to age. For them, the sun
was a farmer's ruddy face, the moon peeped through a cloud
and the Milky Way gladdened them like a birch-lined road.
They longed for the Kingdom which is always near,
always right at hand. Then, under apple trees
angels in homespun linen will come parting the boughs
and at the white kolkhoz tablecloth
cordiality and affection will feast (falling to the ground at times).

And you are from surf-rattled skerries. From the heaths
where burying a warrior they broke his bones
so he could not haunt the living. From the sea night
which your forefathers pulled over themselves, without a word.
Above your head no face, neither the sun's nor the moon's,
only the throbbing of galaxies, the immutable
violence of new beginnings, of new destruction.

All your life listening to the ocean. Black dinosaurs
wade where a purple zone of phosphorescent weeds
rises and falls on the waves as in a dream. And Agamemnon
sails the boiling deep to the steps of the palace
to have his blood gush onto marble. Till mankind passes
and the pure and stony earth is pounded by the ocean.

Thin-lipped, blue-eyed, without grace or hope,
before God the Terrible, body of the world.
Prayers are not heard. Basalt and granite.
Above them, a bird of prey. The only beauty.

What have I to do with you? From footpaths in the orchards,
from an untaught choir and shimmers of a monstrance,

from flower beds of rue, hills by the rivers, books
in which a zealous Lithuanian announced brotherhood, I come.
Oh, consolations of mortals, futile creeds.

And yet you did not know what I know. The earth teaches
More than does the nakedness of elements. No one with impunity
gives to himself the eyes of a god. So brave, in a void,
you offered sacrifices to demons: there were Wotan and Thor,
the screech of Erinyes in the air, the terror of dogs
when Hekate with her retinue of the dead draws near.

Better to carve suns and moons on the joints of crosses
as was done in my district. To birches and firs
give feminine names. To implore protection
against the mute and treacherous might
than to proclaim, as you did, an inhuman thing.

Berkeley, 1963

SENTENCES

What constitutes the training of the hand?
I shall tell what constitutes the training of the hand.
One suspects something is wrong with transcribing signs
But the hand transcribes only the signs it has learned.
Then it is sent to the school of blots and scrawls
Till it forgets what is graceful. For even the sign of a butterfly
Is a well with coiled poisonous smoke inside.

☙

Perhaps we should have represented him otherwise
Than in the form of dove. As fire, yes, but that is beyond us.
For even when it consumes logs on a hearth
We search in it for eyes and hands. Let him then be green,
All blades of calamus, running on footbridges
Over meadows, with a thump of his bare feet. Or in the air
Blowing a birchbark trumpet so strongly that farther down
There tumbles from its blast a crowd of petty officials,
Their uniforms unbuttoned and their women's combs
Flying like chips when the ax strikes.

☙

Still it's just too great a responsibility to lure the souls
From where they lived attentive to the idea of the hummingbird, the
    chair, and the star.
To imprison them within either-or: male sex, female sex,
So that they wake up in the blood of childbirth, crying.

Berkeley, 1963–1965

WINDOW

I looked out the window at dawn and saw a young apple tree translucent in brightness.

And when I looked out at dawn once again, an apple tree laden with fruit stood there.

Many years had probably gone by but I remember nothing of what happened in my sleep.

Berkeley, 1965

WITH TRUMPETS
AND ZITHERS

1
The gift was never named. We lived and a hot light created stood in its
   sphere.
Castles on rocky spurs, herbs in river valleys, descents into the bays
   under ash trees.
All past wars in the flesh, all loves, conch shells of the Celts, Norman
   boats by the cliffs.
Breathing in, breathing out, o Elysium, we would kneel and kiss the
   earth.
A naked girl crossed a town overgrown with green moss and bees
   returned heavy for their evening milking.
Labyrinths of species at our headrest up to the thick of phosphorous
   woods at the entrance of limestone caves.
And in a summer rainstorm putting out paper lanterns on the dark
   village square, couples laughing in flight.
Water steamed at dawn by Calypso's island where an oriole flutters in
   the white crown of a poplar.
I looked at fishermen's dinghies stopped at the other shore and the year
   once again turned over, the vintage season began.

2
I address you, my consciousness, when in a sultry night shot with
   lightnings the plane is landing at Beauvais or Kalamazoo.
And a stewardess moves about quietly so not to wake anyone while the
   cellular wax of cities glimmers beneath.
I believed I would understand but it is late and I know nothing except
   laughter and weeping.
The wet grasses of fertile deltas cleansed me from time and changed all
   into a present without beginning or end.
I disappear in architectural spirals, in lines of a crystal, in the sound of
   instruments playing in forests.
Once again I return to excessive orchards and only the echo seeks me
   in that house on the hill under a hundred-year-old hazel tree.

Then how can you overtake me, you, weighing blame and merit, now
    when I do not remember who I am and who I was?
On many shores at once I am lying cheek on the sand and the same
    ocean runs in, beating its ecstatic drums.

3

And throughout the afternoon the endless talk of cicadas while on the
    slope they are drinking wine from a traveler's goblet.
Fingers ripping at meat, juice trickles on graying beards, a ring perhaps
    or glitter of a gold chain round the neck.
A beauty arrives from canopied beds, from cradles on rockers, washed
    and combed by her mother's hand so that undoing her hair we
    remove a tortoiseshell comb.
Skin scented with oils, arch-browed on city squares, her breasts for our
    cupped hands in the Tigris and Euphrates gardens.
Then they beat on the strings and shout on the heights and below at
    the bend of a river the campground's orange tents slowly surrender
    to shadows.

4

Nothing but laughter and weeping. Terror and no defense and arm in
    arm they drag me to a pit of tangled bones.
Soon I will join their dance, with bailiffs, wenches, and kings, such as
    they used to paint on the tablecloth at our revels.
With a train of my clock carried by the Great Jester, not I, just the
    Sinner to whom a honey-sweet age was brought by winged
    Fortune.
To whom three masked Slavic devils, Duliban, Kostruban, Mendrela,
    squealing and farting, would offer huge smoking plates.
Fingers grabbing at fingers, tongues fornicating with tongues, but not
    mine was the sense of touch, not mine was the knowledge.
Beyond seven rocky mountains I searched for my Teacher and yet I am
    here, not myself, at a pit of tangled bones.

I am standing on a theatrum, astonished by the last things, the puppet
    Death has black ribs and still I cannot believe.

5

The scent of freshly mown clover redeemed the perished armies and
    the meadows glittered in headlights forever.
An immense night of July filled my mouth with a taste of rain and near
    Puybrun by the bridges my childhood was given back.
The warm encampments of crickets chirped under a low cloud just as
    in our lost homelands where a wooden cart goes creaking.
Borne by an inscrutable power, one century gone, I heard, beating in
    darkness, the heart of the dead and the living.

6

What separates, falls. Yet my scream "no!" is still heard though it burned
    out in the wind.
Only what separates does not fall. All the rest is beyond persistence.
I wanted to describe this, not that, basket of vegetables with a
    redheaded doll of a leek laid across it.
And a stocking on the arm of a chair, a dress crumpled as it was, this
    way, no other.
I wanted to describe her, no one else, asleep on her belly, made secure
    by the warmth of his leg.
Also a cat in the unique tower as purring he composes his memorable
    book.
Not ships but one ship with a blue patch in the corner of its sail.
Not streets, for once there was a street with a shop sign: "Schuhmacher
    Pupke."
In vain I tried because what remains is the ever-recurring basket.
And not she whose skin perhaps I, of all men, loved, but a grammatical
    form.
No one cares that precisely this cat wrote *The Adventures of
    Telemachus.*
And the street will always be only one of many streets without name.

7

From a limbo for unbaptized infants and for animal souls let a dead fox
    step out to testify against the language.
Standing for a second in an ant-wing light of pine needles before a boy
    summoned to speak of him forty years later.
Not a general one, a plenipotentiary of the idea of the fox, in his cloak
    lined with the universals.
But he, from a coniferous forest near the village Żegary.
I bring him before the high tribunal in my defense, for what remains
    after desires are doubt and much regret.
And one runs and sails through archipelagoes in the hope of finding a
    place of immutable possession.
Till chandeliers in the rooms of Heloise or Annalena die out and angels
    blow trumpets on the steps of a sculptured bed.
A cheerless dawn advances beyond a palm-lined alley, loudly proclaimed
    by the rattling surf.
And whatever once entered a bolted house of the five senses now is set
    in the brocade of a style.
Which, your honor, does not distinguish particular cases.

8

At dawn the expanse takes its rise, a high horizontal whiteness up to
    the slopes of Tamalpais.
It is torn apart and in the wool of vapor a herd of islands and
    promontories on their watery pastures.
Knife-blue in twilight, a rose-tinted tin, liquid copper, izumrud, smaragdos.
Quiverfuls of buildings touched by a ray: Oakland, San Francisco, before
    the mica in motion lights up below: Berkeley, El Cerrito.
In the oceanic wind eucalyptus husks clashing and disentangling.
Height, length, and width take in their arms a sleeping caterpillar of a
    rolled body.
And carry it over a frozen waste of the Sierras to the most distant
    province of the continent.

Layers of Christmas tinsels wheel round, cities on the bay, buckled by
    luminous ropes of three bridges.
In the hour of ending night it amazes—this place, this time, assigned for
    an awakening of this particular body.

9
I asked what was the day. It was St. Andrew's Eve.
She and her smashed little mirrors under the weeds and snows where
    also the States and banners molder.
Outlandish districts in mud up to the axle-tree, names I alone
    remember: Gineitai, Apýtalaukis.
In the silence of stopped spinning-wheels, fear by the flame of two
    candles, a mouse scratching, a nuptial of phantoms.
In electronic music I heard lugubrious sirens, people's panicky calls
    crushed into flutters and rustles.
I was sitting before a mirror but no hand reached out of darkness to
    touch me on the shoulder.
There, behind me, flash after flash, flocks of birds were taking off from
    the banks of spring ice.
Fanning with their four wings storks stood on their nest in a majestic
    copulation.
My dishonest memory did not preserve anything, save the triumph of
    nameless births.
When I would hear a voice, it seemed to me I distinguished in it words
    of forgiveness.

10
The dream shared at night by all people has inhabitants, hairy animals.
It is a huge and snug forest and everyone entering it walks on all fours
    till dawn through the very thick of the tangle.
Through the wilderness inaccessible to metal objects, all-embracing like
    a warm and deep river.
In satin tunnels the touch distinguishes apples and their color that does
    not recall anything real.

All are quadrupeds, their thighs rejoice at the badger-bear softness, their
   rosy tongues lick each other's fur.
The "I" is felt with amazement in the heartbeat, but so large it cannot
   be filled by the whole Earth with her seasons.
Nor would the skin guarding a different essence trace any boundary.
Later on, in crude light, separated into you and me, they try with a bare
   foot pebbles of the floor.
The two-legged, some to the left, some to the right, put on their belts,
   garters, slacks, and sandals.
And they move on their stilts, longing after a forest home, after low
   tunnels, after an assigned return to it.

II

A coelentera, all pulsating flesh, animal-flower,
All fire, made up of falling bodies joined by the black pin of sex.
It breathes in the center of a galaxy, drawing to itself star after star.
And I, an instant of its duration, on multilaned roads which penetrate
   half-opened mountains.
Bare mountains overgrown with an ageless grass, opened and frozen at a
   sunset before the generations.
Where at large curves one sees nests of cisterns or transparent towers,
   perhaps of missiles.
Along brown leaks by the seashore, rusty stones and butcheries where
   quartered whales are ground to powder.
I wanted to be a judge but those whom I called "they" have changed
   into myself.
I was getting rid of my faith so as not to be better than men and
   women who are certain only of their unknowing.
And on the roads of my terrestrial homeland turning round with the
   music of the spheres
I thought that all I could do would be done better one day.

Berkeley, 1965

WHITENESS

O white, white, white. White city where women carry bread and
    vegetables, women born under the signs of the ever-gyrating
    zodiacs.
The jaws of fountains spout water in the green sun as in the days past of
    nuptials, of strolls in the cold aurora from one outskirt to another.
Buckles from schoolboys' belts somewhere in the dense earth, bunkers
    and sarcophagi bound with blackberry ropes.
Revelations of touch, again and again new beginnings, no knowledge,
    no memory ever accepted.
A faltering passerby, I walk through a street market after the loss of
    speech.
The candlesticks in the conquerors' tents overflow with wax, anger has
    left me and on my tongue the sourness of winter apples.
Two Gypsy women rising from the ashes beat a little drum and dance
    for immortal men.
In a sky inhabited or empty (no one cares) just pigeons and echoes.
Loud is my lament, for I believed despair could last and love could last.
In the white city which does not demand, does not know, does not
    name, but which was and which will be.

Paris, 1966

WHEN THE MOON

When the moon rises and women in flowery dresses are strolling,
I am struck by their eyes, eyelashes, and the whole arrangement of the
    world.
It seems to me that from such a strong mutual attraction
The ultimate truth should issue at last.

Berkeley, 1966

ON THE ROAD

To what summoned? And to whom? blindly, God almighty, through horizons of woolly haze,

Fata morganas of coppery scales on the fortresses of maritime provinces,

Through a smoke of vines burning over creek beds or through the blue myrrh of dimmed churches,

To the unattainable, small valley, shaded forever by words, where the two of us, naked and kneeling, are cleansed by an unreal spring.

Without the apple of knowledge, on long loops from earth to sky, from sky to the dried blood of potter's soil.

Disinherited of prophecies, eating bread at noon under a tall pine stronger than any hope.

St.-Paul-de-Vence, 1967

INCANTATION

Human reason is beautiful and invincible.
No bars, no barbed wire, no pulping of books,
No sentence of banishment can prevail against it.
It establishes the universal ideas in language,
And guides our hand so we write Truth and Justice
With capital letters, lie and oppression with small.
It puts what should be above things as they are,
Is an enemy of despair and a friend of hope.
It does not know Jew from Greek or slave from master,
Giving us the estate of the world to manage.
It saves austere and transparent phrases
From the filthy discord of tortured words.
It says that everything is new under the sun,
Opens the congealed fist of the past.
Beautiful and very young are Philo-Sophia
And poetry, her ally in the service of the good.
As late as yesterday Nature celebrated their birth,
The news was brought to the mountains by a unicorn and an echo.
Their friendship will be glorious, their time has no limit.
Their enemies have delivered themselves to destruction.

Berkeley, 1968

ARS POETICA?

I have always aspired to a more spacious form
that would be free from the claims of poetry or prose
and would let us understand each other without exposing
the author or reader to sublime agonies.

In the very essence of poetry there is something indecent:
a thing is brought forth which we didn't know we had in us,
so we blink our eyes, as if a tiger had sprung out
and stood in the light, lashing his tail.

That's why poetry is rightly said to be dictated by a daimonion,
though it's an exaggeration to maintain that he must be an angel.
It's hard to guess where that pride of poets comes from,
when so often they're put to shame by the disclosure of their frailty.

What reasonable man would like to be a city of demons,
who behave as if they were at home, speak in many tongues,
and who, not satisfied with stealing his lips or hand,
work at changing his destiny for their convenience?

It's true that what is morbid is highly valued today,
and so you may think that I am only joking
or that I've devised just one more means
of praising Art with the help of irony.

There was a time when only wise books were read,
helping us to bear our pain and misery.
This, after all, is not quite the same
as leafing through a thousand works fresh from psychiatric clinics.

And yet the world is different from what it seems to be
and we are other than how we see ourselves in our ravings.

People therefore preserve silent integrity,
thus earning the respect of their relatives and neighbors.

The purpose of poetry is to remind us
how difficult it is to remain just one person,
for our house is open, there are no keys in the doors,
and invisible guests come in and out at will.

What I'm saying here is not, I agree, poetry,
as poems should be written rarely and reluctantly,
under unbearable duress and only with the hope
that good spirits, not evil ones, choose us for their instrument.

Berkeley, 1968

MY FAITHFUL MOTHER TONGUE

Faithful mother tongue,
I have been serving you.
Every night, I used to set before you little bowls of colors
so you could have your birch, your cricket, your finch
as preserved in my memory.

This lasted many years.
You were my native land; I lacked any other.
I believed that you would also be a messenger
between me and some good people
even if they were few, twenty, ten
or not born, as yet.

Now, I confess my doubt.
There are moments when it seems to me I have squandered my life.
For you are a tongue of the debased,
of the unreasonable, hating themselves
even more than they hate other nations,
a tongue of informers,
a tongue of the confused,
ill with their own innocence.

But without you, who am I?
Only a scholar in a distant country,
a success, without fears and humiliations.
Yes, who am I without you?
Just a philosopher, like everyone else.

I understand, this is meant as my education:
the glory of individuality is taken away,
Fortune spreads a red carpet

before the sinner in a morality play
while on the linen backdrop a magic lantern throws
images of human and divine torture.

Faithful mother tongue,
perhaps after all it's I who must try to save you.
So I will continue to set before you little bowls of colors
bright and pure if possible,
for what is needed in misfortune is a little order and beauty.

Berkeley, 1968

CITY WITHOUT A NAME

I

Who will honor the city without a name
If so many are dead and others pan gold
Or sell arms in faraway countries?

What shepherd's horn swathed in the bark of birch
Will sound in the Ponary Hills the memory of the absent—
Vagabonds, Pathfinders, brethren of a dissolved lodge?

This spring, in a desert, beyond a campsite flagpole,
—In silence that stretched to the solid rock of yellow and red
     mountains—
I heard in a gray bush the buzzing of wild bees.

The current carried an echo and the timber of rafts.
A man in a visored cap and a woman in a kerchief
Pushed hard with their four hands at a heavy steering oar.

In the library, below a tower painted with the signs of the zodiac,
Kontrym would take a whiff from his snuffbox and smile
For despite Metternich all was not yet lost.

And on crooked lanes down the middle of a sandy highway
Jewish carts went their way while a black grouse hooted
Standing on a cuirassier's helmet, a relict of La Grande Armée.

2

In Death Valley I thought about styles of hairdo,
About a hand that shifted spotlights at the Students' Ball
In the city from which no voice could reach me.
Minerals did not sound the last trumpet.
There was only the rustle of a loosened grain of lava.

In Death Valley salt gleams from a dried-up lake bed.
Defend, defend yourself, says the tick-tock of the blood.
From the futility of solid rock, no wisdom.

In Death Valley no hawk or eagle against the sky.
The prediction of a Gypsy woman has come true.
In a lane under an arcade, then, I was reading a poem
Of someone who had lived next door, entitled "An Hour of
    Thought."

I looked long at the rearview mirror: there, the one man
Within three hundred miles, an Indian, was walking a bicycle uphill.

3
With flutes, with torches
And a drum, boom, boom,
Look, the one who died in Istanbul, there, in the first row.
He walks arm in arm with his young lady,
And over them swallows fly.

They carry oars or staffs garlanded with leaves
And bunches of flowers from the shores of the Green Lakes,
As they come closer and closer, down Castle Street.
And then suddenly nothing, only a white puff of cloud
Over the Humanities Students Club,
Division of Creative Writing.

4
Books, we have written a whole library of them.
Lands, we have visited a great many of them.
Battles, we have lost a number of them.
Till we are no more, we and our Maryla.

5

Understanding and pity,
We value them highly.
What else?

Beauty and kisses,
Fame and its prizes,
Who cares?

Doctors and lawyers,
Well–turned–out majors,
Six feet of earth.

Rings, furs, and lashes,
Glances at Masses,
Rest in peace.

Sweet twin breasts, good night.
Sleep through to the light,
Without spiders.

6

The sun goes down above the Zealous Lithuanian Lodge
And kindles fire on landscapes "made from nature":
The Wilia winding among pines; black honey of the Żejmiana;
The Mereczanka washes berries near the Żegaryno village.
The valets had already brought in Theban candelabra
And pulled curtains, one after the other, slowly,
While, thinking I entered first, taking off my gloves,
I saw that all the eyes were fixed on me.

7

When I got rid of grieving
And the glory I was seeking,
Which I had no business doing,

I was carried by dragons
Over countries, bays, and mountains,
By fate, or by what happens.

Oh yes, I wanted to be me.
I toasted mirrors weepily
And learned my own stupidity.

From nails, mucous membrane,
Lungs, liver, bowels, and spleen
Whose house is made? Mine.

So what else is new?
I am not my own friend.
Time cuts me in two.

Monuments covered with snow,
Accept my gift. I wandered;
And where, I don't know.

8
Absent, burning, acrid, salty, sharp.
Thus the feast of Insubstantiality.
Under a gathering of clouds anywhere.
In a bay, on a plateau, in a dry arroyo.
No density. No hardness of stone.
Even the *Summa* thins into straw and smoke.
And the angelic choirs fly over in a pomegranate seed
Sounding every few instants, not for us, their trumpets.

9
Light, universal, and yet it keeps changing.
For I love the light too, perhaps the light only.

Yet what is too dazzling and too high is not for me.
So when the clouds turn rosy, I think of light that is level
In the lands of birch and pine coated with crispy lichen,
Late in autumn, under the hoarfrost when the last milk caps
Rot under the firs and the hounds' barking echoes,
And jackdaws wheel over the tower of a Basilian church.

10

Unexpressed, untold.
But how?
The shortness of life,
the years quicker and quicker,
not remembering whether it happened in this or that autumn.
Retinues of homespun velveteen skirts,
giggles above a railing, pigtails askew,
sittings on chamberpots upstairs
when the sledge jingles under the columns of the porch
just before the moustachioed ones in wolf fur enter.
Female humanity,
children's snot, legs spread apart,
snarled hair, the milk boiling over,
stench, shit frozen into clods.
And those centuries,
conceiving in the herring smell of the middle of the night
instead of playing something like a game of chess
or dancing an intellectual ballet.
And palisades,
and pregnant sheep,
and pigs, fast eaters and poor eaters,
and cows cured by incantations.

11

Not the Last Judgment, just a kermess by a river.
Small whistles, clay chickens, candied hearts.

So we trudged through the slush of melting snow
To buy bagels from the district of Smorgonie.

A fortune-teller hawking: "Your destiny, your planets."
And a toy devil bobbing in a tube of crimson brine.
Another, a rubber one, expired in the air squeaking,
By the stand where you bought stories of King Otto and Melusine.

12

Why should that city, defenseless and pure as the wedding necklace of a forgotten tribe, keep offering itself to me?

Like blue and red-brown seeds beaded in Tuzigoot in the copper desert seven centuries ago.

Where ocher rubbed into stone still waits for the brow and cheekbone it would adorn, though for all that time there has been no one.

What evil in me, what pity has made me deserve this offering?

It stands before me, ready, not even the smoke from one chimney is lacking, not one echo, when I step across the rivers that separate us.

Perhaps Anna and Dora Drużyno have called to me, three hundred miles inside Arizona, because except for me no one else knows that they ever lived.

They trot before me on Embankment Street, two gently born parakeets from Samogitia, and at night they unravel for me their spinster tresses of gray hair.

Here there is no earlier and no later; the seasons of the year and of the day are simultaneous.

At dawn shit-wagons leave town in long rows and municipal employees at the gate collect the turnpike toll in leather bags.

Rattling their wheels, "Courier" and "Speedy" move against the current to Werki, and an oarsman shot down over England skiffs past, spread-eagled by his oars.

At St. Peter and Paul's the angels lower their thick eyelids in a smile over a nun who has indecent thoughts.

Bearded, in a wig, Mrs. Sora Klok sits at the counter, instructing her twelve shopgirls.

And all of German Street tosses into the air unfurled bolts of fabric, pre-paring itself for death and the conquest of Jerusalem.

Black and princely, an underground river knocks at cellars of the cathedral under the tomb of St. Casimir the Young and under the half-charred oak logs in the hearth.

Carrying her servant's-basket on her shoulder, Barbara, dressed in mourning, returns from the Lithuanian Mass at St. Nicholas to the Romers' house on Bakszta Street.

How it glitters! the snow on Three Crosses Hill and Bekiesz Hill, not to be melted by the breath of these brief lives.

And what do I know now, when I turn into Arsenal Street and open my eyes once more on a useless end of the world?

I was running, as the silks rustled, through room after room without stopping, for I believed in the existence of a last door.

But the shape of lips and an apple and a flower pinned to a dress were all that one was permitted to know and take away.

The Earth, neither compassionate nor evil, neither beautiful nor atrocious, persisted, innocent, open to pain and desire.

And the gift was useless, if, later on, in the flarings of distant nights, there was not less bitterness but more.

If I cannot so exhaust my life and their life that the bygone crying is transformed, at last, into a harmony.

Like a *Noble Jan Dęboróg* in the Straszun's secondhand-book shop, I am put to rest forever between two familiar names.

The castle tower above the leafy tumulus grows small and there is still a hardly audible—is it Mozart's *Requiem?*—music.

In the immobile light I move my lips and perhaps I am even glad not to find the desired word.

Berkeley, 1968

TO RAJA RAO

Raja, I wish I knew
the cause of that malady.

For years I could not accept
the place I was in.
I felt I should be somewhere else.

A city, trees, human voices
lacked the quality of presence.
I would live by the hope of moving on.

Somewhere else there was a city of real presence,
of real trees and voices and friendship and love.

Link, if you wish, my peculiar case
(on the border of schizophrenia)
to the messianic hope
of my civilization.

Ill at ease in the tyranny, ill at ease in the republic,
in the one I longed for freedom, in the other for the end of corruption.

Building in my mind a permanent polis
forever deprived of aimless bustle.

I learned at last to say: this is my home,
here, before the glowing coal of ocean sunsets,
on the shore which faces the shores of your Asia,
in a great republic, moderately corrupt.

Raja, this did not cure me
of my guilt and shame.

A shame of failing to be
what I should have been.

The image of myself
grows gigantic on the wall
and against it
my miserable shadow.

That's how I came to believe
in Original Sin
which is nothing but the first
victory of the ego.

Tormented by my ego, deluded by it
I give you, as you see, a ready argument.

I hear you saying that liberation is possible
and that Socratic wisdom
is identical with your guru's.

No, Raja, I must start from what I am.
I am those monsters which visit my dreams
and reveal to me my hidden essence.

If I am sick, there is no proof whatsoever
that man is a healthy creature.

Greece had to lose, her pure consciousness
had to make our agony only more acute.

We needed God loving us in our weakness
and not in the glory of beatitude.

No help, Raja, my part is agony,
struggle, abjection, self-love, and self-hate,
prayer for the Kingdom
and reading Pascal.

Berkeley, 1969

SO LITTLE

I said so little.
Days were short.

Short days.
Short nights.
Short years.

I said so little.
I couldn't keep up.

My heart grew weary
From joy,
Despair,
Ardor,
Hope.

The jaws of Leviathan
Were closing upon me.

Naked, I lay on the shores
Of desert islands.

The white whale of the world
Hauled me down to its pit.

And now I don't know
What in all that was real.

Berkeley, 1969

SEASONS

Transparent tree, full of migrating birds on a blue morning,
Cold because there is still snow in the mountains.

Berkeley, 1971

GIFT

A day so happy.
Fog lifted early, I worked in the garden.
Hummingbirds were stopping over honeysuckle flowers.
There was no thing on earth I wanted to possess.
I knew no one worth my envying him.
Whatever evil I had suffered, I forgot.
To think that once I was the same man did not embarrass me.
In my body I felt no pain.
When straightening up, I saw the blue sea and sails.

Berkeley, 1971

FROM THE RISING OF THE SUN

I. The Unveiling

Whatever I hold in my hand, a stylus, reed, quill or a ballpoint,
Wherever I may be, on the tiles of an atrium, in a cloister cell, in a hall
    before the portrait of a king,
I attend to matters I have been charged with in the provinces.
And I begin, though nobody can explain why and wherefore.
Just as I do now, under a dark-blue cloud with a glint of the red horse.
Retainers are busy, I know, in underground chambers,
Rustling rolls of parchment, preparing colored ink and sealing wax.

This time I am frightened. Odious rhythmic speech
Which grooms itself and, of its own accord, moves on.
Even if I wanted to stop it, weak as I am from fever,
Because of a flu like the last one that brought mournful revelations
When, looking at the futility of my ardent years,
I heard a storm from the Pacific beating against the window.
But no, gird up your loins, pretend to be brave to the end
Because of daylight and the neighing of the red horse.

Vast lands. Flickering of hazy trains.
Children walk by an open field, all is gray beyond an Estonian village.
Royza, captain of the cavalry. Mowczan. Angry gales.
Never again will I kneel in my small country, by a river,
So that what is stone in me could be dissolved,
So that nothing would remain but my tears, tears.

CHORUS:
Hope of old people,
Never assuaged.
They wait for their day
Of power and glory.

For a day of comprehension.
They have so much to accomplish

In a month, in a year,
To the end.

It rolls along, sky-like, in the sun on its islands, in the flow of salty
   breezes.
It flies past and does not, new and the same.
Narrow sculptured boats, a hundred oars, on the stern a dancer
Beats baton against baton, flinging his knees.
Sonorous pagodas, beasts in pearl-studded nets,
Hidden staircases of princesses, floodgates, gardens of lilies.
It rolls along, it flies by, our speech.

CHORUS:
He whose life was short can easily be forgiven.
He whose life was long can hardly be forgiven.
When will that shore appear from which at last we see
How all this came to pass and for what reason?

Darkly, darkly cities return.
The roads of a twenty-year-old are littered with maple leaves
As he walks along one acrid morning, looking through the fences at
   gardens
And courtyards, where a black dog barks, and someone chops wood.

Now on a bridge he listens to the babble of the river, bells are
   resounding.
Under the pines of sandy bluffs he hears echoes, sees white frost and
   fog.

How did I come to know the scent of smoke, of late autumn dahlias
On the sloping little streets of a wooden town

Since it was so long ago, in a millennium visited in dreams
Far from here, in a light of which I am uncertain?

Was I there, cuddled like a vegetal baby in a seed,
Called long before the hours, one after another, would touch me?
Does so little remain of our labors lasting till evening
That we have nothing left except our completed fate?

Under the dark-blue cloud with a glint of the red horse
I dimly recognize all that has been.
The clothes of my name fall away and disappear.
The stars in wide waters grow smaller.
Again the other, unnamed one, speaks for me.
And he opens fading dream-like houses
So that I write here in desolation
Beyond the land and sea.

II. Diary of a Naturalist

In search of a four-leaf clover through the meadows at dawn,
In search of a double hazelnut into deep forest.
There we were promised a great, great life
And it waited, though we weren't yet born.

The oak our father, rough was his shoulder.
Sister birch led us with a whisper.
Farther and farther we went on to meet
The living water in which all strength revives.

Until, wandering through a dense black forest
All the long day of a young summer,
We will come at dusk to the edge of bright waters
Where the king of beavers rules over the crossings.

Fare well, Nature.
Fare well, Nature.

We were flying over a range of snowpeaked mountains
And throwing dice for the soul of the condor.
—Should we grant reprieve to the condor?
—No, we won't grant reprieve to the condor.
It didn't eat from the Tree of Knowledge and so it must perish.

In a park by a river a bear blocked our way
And extending his paw begged for assistance.
—Was it this one that frightened lost travelers?
—Let's give him a bottle of beer to cheer him up.
Once he had treefuls of honey on his estates.

He loped gracefully across an asphalt freeway
And once more a wood misty with rain moved past in our lights.
—It looked like a cougar.
—That would make sense.
They should be here according to statistics.

Fare well, Nature.
Fare well, Nature.

I show here how my childish dream was denied:

And now, on my school bench but not present, I slip into a picture on a wall in the classroom, "Animals of North America."

Fraternizing with the raccoon, stroking the wapiti, chasing wild swans over a caribou trail.

The wilderness protects me, there a gray squirrel can walk for weeks on the treetops.

But I will be called to the blackboard, and who can guess when, in what years.

The chalk breaks in my fingers, I turn around and hear a voice, mine, probably mine:

"White as horse skulls in the desert, black as a trail of interplanetary night

Nakedness, nothing more, a cloudless picture of Motion.

It was Eros who plaited garlands of fruit and flowers,

Who poured dense gold from a pitcher into sunrises and sunsets.

He and no one else led us into fragrant landscapes

Of branches hanging low by streams, of gentle hills,

And an echo lured us on and on, a cuckoo promised

A place, deep in a thicket, where there is no longing.

Our eyes were touched: instead of decay, the green,

The cinnabar of a tiger lily, the bitter blue of a gentian,

Furriness of bark in half-shade, a marten flickered,

Yes, only delight, Eros. Should we then trust

The alchemy of blood, marry forever the childish earth of illusion?

Or bear a naked light without color, without speech,

That demands nothing from us and calls us nowhere?"

I covered my face with my hands and those sitting on the benches kept silent.

They were unknown to me, for my age was over and my generation lost.

I tell about my acumen at a time when, guessing a few things in advance, I hit upon an idea, certainly not new, but highly regarded by my betters about whom I knew nothing:

> My generation was lost. Cities too. And nations.
> But all this a little later. Meanwhile, in the window, a swallow
> Performs its rite of an instant. That boy, does he already suspect
> That beauty is always elsewhere and always delusive?
> Now he sees his homeland. At the time of the second mowing.
> Roads winding uphill and down. Pine groves. Lakes.
> An overcast sky with one slanting ray.
> And everywhere men with scythes, in shirts of unbleached linen
> And the dark-blue trousers that were common in the province.
> He sees what I see even now. Oh but he was clever,
> Attentive, as if things were instantly changed by memory.
> Riding in a cart, he looked back to retain as much as possible.
> Which means he knew what was needed for some ultimate
>   moment
> When he would compose from fragments a world perfect at last.

Everything would be fine if language did not deceive us by finding different names for the same thing in different times and places:

> The Alpine shooting star, *Dodecatheon alpinum,*
> Grows in the mountain woods over Rogue River,
> Which river, in southern Oregon,
> Owing to its rocky, hardly accessible banks,
> Is a river of fishermen and hunters. The black bear and the cougar
> Are still relatively common on these slopes.

The plant was so named for its pink-purple flowers
Whose slanting tips point to the ground from under the petals,
And resembles a star from nineteenth-century illustrations
That falls, pulling along a thin sheaf of lines.
The name was given to the river by French trappers
When one of them stumbled into an Indian ambush.
From that time on they called it La Rivière des Coquins,
The River of Scoundrels, or Rogue, in translation.
I sat by its loud and foamy current
Tossing in pebbles and thinking that the name
Of that flower in the Indian language will never be known,
No more than the native name of their river.
A word should be contained in every single thing
But it is not. So what then of my vocation?

Nonsensical stanzas intrude, about Anusia and *żalia rutéle,* or green rue, always, it
seems, a symbol of life and happiness:

Why did Anusia grow that rue
The evergreen rue in her maiden's garden?
And why did she sing of *żalia rutéle*
So that evening echoes carried over the water?

And where did she go in her wreath of fresh rue?
Did she take the skirt from her coffer when leaving?
And who will know her in the Indian beyond
When her name was Anusia and she is no more?

I give a brief account of what happened to a book which was once my favorite,
Our Forest and Its Inhabitants:

The lament of a slaughtered hare fills the forest.
It fills the forest and disturbs nothing there.
For the dying of a particular being is its own private business

And everyone has to cope with it in whatever way he can.
Our Forest and Its Inhabitants. Our, of our village,
Fenced in with a wire. Sucking, munching, digesting,
Growing, and being annihilated. A callous mother.
If the wax in our ears could melt, a moth on pine needles,
A beetle half-eaten by a bird, a wounded lizard
Would all lie at the center of the expanding circles
Of their vibrating agony. That piercing sound
Would drown out the loud shots of bursting seeds and buds,
And our child who gathers wild strawberries in a basket.
Would not hear the trilling, nice after all, of the thrush.

I pay homage to Stefan Bagiński who taught me how to operate a microscope
and prepare a slide. Nor am I forgetting about the main contributor to my
pessimism, and even quote from a work about his deeds in the service of science,
published for the use of young people in the year 1890 in Warsaw: Prof. Erazm
Majewski, *Doctor Catchfly; Fantastic Adventures in the World of Insects:*

To the masters of our youth, greetings.
To you, my teacher, Mr. Life Science,
Spleeny Bagiński in checkered knickers,
The ruler of *infusoria* and amoebas.
Wherever your skull with its woolly tuft
Reposes, rocked by the whirling elements,
Whatever fate befell your glasses
In their gold-wire rims,
I offer you these words.

And to you, Doctor Catchfly,
Who are free from destruction, the hero
Of a historic expedition to the land of insects.
You live as always on Miodowa in Warsaw
And your servant Gregory dusts carpets every morning,

While you set off on your old bachelor's walk
Through the park, the place of your victory
Over all things subject to ruin and change.

It happened in the summer of the year 187*:

"The day when our naturalist was to lead his beautiful fiancée to the altar was calm, sunny and without a breeze. Precisely the kind of day needed for a specimen-gathering expedition. But Dr. Catchfly, already dressed in his frock-coat, was not thinking of two-winged creatures. Attracted by the fine weather and faithful to his habits, he simply decided to spend his last free hour in the Park of the Royal Baths. While walking, he was meditating on the happiness of their future life together when suddenly something flickered before his dreamy eyes: a tiny little two-winged thing. He glanced and stopped, dumbfounded. Before him was a robber fly, but one that he had never seen before! His heart began pounding. He held his breath and drew closer to the leaf in order to better observe this rare specimen. But the wary insect, allowing him just enough time to make sure it was indeed extraordinary, flew off to another branch. Our naturalist, his eyes fixed on the insect, approached on tiptoe but the robber fly, quite smart, it seems, took its leave in time. This was repeated a few times and the frolicsome fly led him to the other side of the flower bed. The naturalist was losing it from sight and finding it again, while time passed. The hour of the wedding arrived but the robber fly placed itself very high, so high, as a matter of fact, that to keep it in sight, it was necessary to climb the tree. There was not a moment to lose."

Ah, subterfuges of Fate! That he was caught
Stalking on a branch, exactly when extending his top hat.
That when hearing this news, the maiden swooned.

She was an unreasonable creature of the fairer sex.
She chose her Earth of tulle and gauze,

Of boudoir mirrors that were easily cracked,
Of faience chamberpots that leave only one ear
To the excavator's shovel. The Earth of midwives, mourners,
Of whispers *Between the Lips and the Cup,*
Or else between lips and a pastry
Devoured in wastelands by posthumous descendants.
An ordinary earth, after all. Priceless for many.
Oh may the earth lie lightly on her, though light it is never.
If not for that day, admit it, John Catchfly,
Your zeal would have grown tame among lampshades.
A passion, pure and manifest,
Would not have led you to your destiny,
Until at dawn on a meadow in the Tatra mountains,
In the Valley of White Water and Rówienka,
Looking at the red of the rising sun,
Obedient to the formula, you drank the elixir
And went down to where there is neither guilt nor complaint.

Tiny, I wandered with you in the unfathomed land
Beneath stalks of grass as thick as cedars,
In the din and blast of diaphanous, winged machines.
I would stand in the middle of a rugged leaf
And over the gloom of a swampy chasm
I pulled myself along a strand of gossamer.

You wrote down: "horrible conditions."
In sap, mush, glue, millions and millions
Of entangled legs, wings, and abdomens
Struggle to free themselves, weaken, stiffen forever.
The fat flesh of caterpillars being devoured alive
By the rapacious progeny of inquisitive flies,
Undulates its segments, and grazes unconcerned.
O humanitarian from the age of debates,

What sort of scientist are you, why do you feel compassion?
Is it proper to suddenly get incensed
When on a black, smoldering plain
You arrive at the gates of a burned-down city,
Witness and judge in a hall of dead ants?

You infected me with your pity for computers
Dressed in chitin cloaks, in transparent armor.
And in my child's imagination
I still bear your mark, O philosopher of pain.
But I don't hold a grudge, Dr. *honoris causa*
Of Heidelberg and Jena. I am glad
That the white of the ivory on your cane still shines
As if it has never been dimmed by fire
And someone still rode in carriages down the avenues.

I try to describe concisely what I experienced when instead of choosing the
profession of a traveler-naturalist I turned toward other goals:

That's probably why I went on a pilgrimage.
The direction those will recognize who, for instance,
Having visited the caves near Les Eyzies,
Stopping perhaps at noon in Sarlat,
From there took the road that leads to Souillac
Where a bas-relief in a Romanesque portal
Tells the adventures of Monk Theophilus
From Adana in Cilicia, and where the prophet Isaiah
For eight centuries has persisted in a violent gesture
As if he were plucking the strings of an invisible harp.
And on and on, into winding dells, until suddenly
It appears high, so high, that jewel of wayfarers,
As desired as a nest in the top of a fir tree
Was in our boyhood: Roc Amadour.

But I'm not insistent. A road to Compostela
Or to Jasna Góra would instruct you as well.

Pursuing and passing by. Here a mossy rock
Runs, becomes more distinct at every curve,
Then fades in the distance. There, a river flashes
Beyond the trees and the arc of a bridge. But, remember,
Neither the view will stop us, nor the kingfisher
Stitching together the two banks with the bright thread of its flight,
Nor the maiden in the tower, though she lures us with a smile
And blindfolds us before she leads us to her chamber.
I was a patient pilgrim. And so I notched
Each month and year on my stick, since it neared me to my aim.

Yet when at last I arrived after many years
What happened there, many would know, I think,
Who in the parking lot at Roc Amadour
Found a space and then counted the steps
To the upper chapel, to make sure that this was it,
And saw a wooden Madonna with a child in a crown,
Surrounded by a throng of impassive art lovers.
As I did. Not a step further. Mountains and valleys
Crossed. Through flames. Wide waters. And unfaithful memory.
The same passion but I hear no call.
And the holy had its abode only in denial.

. . .

IV. Over Cities

I
If I am responsible
It is not for everything.
I didn't support the theses of Copernicus.
I was neither for nor against in Galileo's case.
My ships have never left the pond to sail the seas.

When I was born, locomotives ran on rails
Moving in a jumble of wheels and pistons,
And the echo of an express train rang wide
Through forests no longer primeval.
The district was inhabited by folk, Jews, and gentry.
You went by horse cart to buy kerosene, herring, and salt,
But in the towns they were using electricity.
It was said that someone had invented the wireless telegraph.
Books were already written. Ideas thoroughly discussed.
The ax was put to the tree.

2

"He that leadeth into captivity, shall go into captivity": thus began my age on the planet Earth. Later on I became a teacher in a city by a great sea and I had just turned away from the blackboard on which they could read, scribbled in my crooked writing: "Maximus the Confessor" and the dates "580–662." A multitude of their faces before me, these boys and girls, born when I was composing the first stanza of a threnody to be read at a memorial service, grew up before I managed to finish the poem. Then, putting aside my chalk, I addressed them in the following words:

"Yes, it is undeniable that extraordinary fates befell our species, precisely those from which Maximus the Confessor wanted to protect us, suspecting as he did the devilish temptation in the truth of reason. Yet while we hear everyone advising us to understand clearly causes and effects, let us beware of those perfectly logical though somewhat too eager arguments. Certainly, it is distressing not to know where this force that carries us away comes from or where it leads. But let us observe restraint and limit ourselves to statements which in our intention will be statements and nothing else. Let us formulate it thus: yes, the Universal is devouring the Particular, our fingers are heavy with Chinese and Assyrian rings, civilizations are as short-lived as weeks of our lives, places which not long ago were celebrated as homelands under oak trees are now no more than States on a map, and each day we ourselves lose letter after letter from our names which still distinguish us from each other."

3

Once upon a time they inhabited the land. The high and low sun
    divided their year.
In fog and mist after St. Michael's, when the angel announces to the
    seed,

Through the four Sundays of Advent and Ember days
Until the blind, the lame, and the crippled rejoice, the power
   trembles,
The sages of the world trudge through the snow protecting myrrh,
   frankincense, and gold.
Frost makes the trees crack in the woods, candles are brought home
   on Candlemas,
He wanders by Genezaret, time for their bearish dances.
The double bass and the drum at Shrovetide until Ash Wednesday.
And lo our little sun //warms the frozen earth again
Riding past green corn //palm in hand //the King enters Jerusalem.

4
It is a ship in the likeness of a trireme or an Egyptian sailboat.

In any case the same as in the days when gods used to call from island to
island, their hands cupped to their mouths.

Driven by a small motor, it comes near on a Pacific swell.

And in the rustle of the surf, runs aground high on the beach.

They are running, a crowd of them. On the deck, on the mast, their
motley nakedness.

Until the whole ship is covered with a swarm opening and closing its
wings,

With men and women from the end of the twentieth century.

Waking up I understood the meaning or, rather, I almost did.

5
A life unendurable but it was endured.
Cattle being driven to pasture in early spring. Speech betrays me here:

I don't know what to call a strip of land fenced with poles
That leads from the last huts of the village up to the forest.
(I have always lacked words and have not been a poet
If a poet is supposed to take pleasure in words.)
So, here is the eldest shepherd and his bags,
And his cross-gartered legs and the longest whipstock.
Two striplings with him. One is carrying a birch-bark trumpet,
The other an old-fashioned pistol, its barrel fixed with a string.
Really seen. Near Širvintai or Grinkiškai.
Long before I entered the monastery,
The light over an always radiant sandstone column,
The same today as in the time of Franconian kings,
Because I wanted to earn a day of comprehension,
Or even a single second, when those three
Would also reveal themselves, each in his unique essence.

6
I was long in learning to speak, now I let days pass without a word.

Incessantly astonished by the day of my birth, once only from the beginning to the end of time.

Born of a foolhardy woman with whom I am united, and whom I, an old man, pity in my dreams.

Her funny dresses, her dances, so utterly lost yet so close again.

And to call her a different name than I called her once, childishly unique.

Means to gauge, forget, number myself as well.

O what happened and when to *principium individuationis*?

Where is the calamus by the river with its scent, mine alone, and for no
one else?

Through what meadows burned brown does she run with me in her
arms

Carrying me to safety, away from the teeth of a beast?

My memory is shut, I don't know who I really was.

Have I fulfilled anything, have I been of use to anyone?

And she, who offered me to Our Lady of Ostrabrama,

How and why was she granted what she asked for in her prayer?

A handless performer with his collection of butterflies,

A fisherman by a lake, proud of his nets, the best in the county,

A gardener growing plants from beyond the seas.

Everything taken away. Crossed out. All our treasures.

So that we are alone at the trial in the dark

And hear her steps nearby, and think she has forgiven.

7
Sir Hieronymus took me by the arm and led me to the park
Where, at the turn of the lane, before a moss-covered Ceres,
A view opened upon meadows, the river, and the whole valley
Up to the towers of a church in the town beyond the forest.
And he was snapping his snuffbox and unhurriedly telling

Of his adventures in St. Petersburg or Naples,
Wittily describing the various countries.
He dealt at length with the swamps of Polesine
Which he once crossed on his way to Ravenna
From Venice, and argued that Jesuits from that province
Named similar Lithuanian swamps: Polesia.
Then he reminisced about Count de Saint-Germain
Or about the lost Book of Hieroglyphic Figures.
Just then the sun was setting over our land.
And he had hardly put his handkerchief into his pocket
When the birds began to sing as in early morning
And the full light of daybreak burst into noon.
Quicker and quicker. A century in half an hour.
And where is Sir Hieronymus? Where did I go? Here there is no one.

V. A Short Recess

I
Life was impossible, but it was endured.
Whose life? Mine, but what does that mean?

During recess, biting into a sandwich wrapped in paper
I stand under the wall in chubby meditation.

And I would have been someone I have never been.
And I would have obtained what I have never obtained.
Jackdaws beyond the window would have been remembered
By another I, not the one in whose words I am thinking now.

And if they say that all I heard was the rushing of a Heraclitean river
That will be enough, for the mere listening to it wore me down.
Scribes in dim rooms calculated on their abacuses.
Or perhaps men drove herds amid the smoke of distant fires.

Abandoned clothes kept for a moment the shape of arms and shoulders.
Pine needles fell onto a plush teddy bear.
And already new peoples with their numerous carts and a cannon.
What else could I be concerned with in Ostrogothic camps?

If only my early love had come true.
If only I had been happy walking down Harbor Street
(Which, anyway, did not lead to a harbor
But only to wet logs beyond the sawmills).
Had I been counted among the elders of our city,
And traveled abroad on an assignment.
Had we concluded an alliance with Ferrara.

Whoever is born just once on earth
Could have been that man whom Isis visited in a dream
And have gone through an initiation
To say afterward: I saw.
I saw the radiant sun at midnight.
I trod Proserpina's threshold.
I passed through all the elements and returned.
I came into the presence of the gods below and the gods above
And adored them face to face.

Or a gladiator, a slave
Under an inscription on a level stone:
"i was not, i was, i am not, i do not desire."

2
—Most distinguished voyager, from where do you hail?

—My city, in a valley among wooded hills
Under a fortified castle at the meeting of two rivers,
Was famous for its ornate temples:
Churches, Catholic and Orthodox, synagogues and mosques.

Our country cultivated rye and flax, it rafted timber as well.
Our army was composed of a lancer regiment,
Dragoons and a regiment of Tartar horsemen.
The postal stamps of our State
Represented phantasms
Sculpted long ago by two artists,
Friends or enemies, Pietro and Giovanni.
Our schools taught dogmatics,
Apologetics, sentences from the Talmud and Titus Livius.
Aristotle was highly regarded,
Though not as highly as sack races and jumping over fires
On Saint John's Eve.

—Most distinguished voyager, what was your eon like?

—Comic. Terror is forgotten.
Only the ridiculous is remembered by posterity.
Death from a wound, from a noose, from starvation
Is one death, but folly is uncounted and new every year.
I took part, I tied neckties
For no purpose and danced dances for no purpose.
A customer, a buyer of sweaters and pomade,
A mimicker, a shy guest,
A fop impressed by his reflection in shop windows.
I was overgrown by the bark of unconsciousness.
I tried hard to imagine another earth and could not.
I tried hard to imagine another heaven and could not.

3
There is an understanding and a covenant
Between all those whom time has defeated and released.
They tap their hammers, put curl paper in their hair,
Walk crooked sidewalks on urgent errands.
Cripples, harlots, swindlers, potentates.

And the duration of their city has no end,
Though they will no longer buy or sell
Nor take for themselves a husband or wife,
In mirrors they are not visible to themselves, or to anyone.
Their linen, wool, calico, and sateen
Sent back to them, as it should be, a little later,
Roll up and shimmer and gently rustle
Under the immovable light of street lamps or sun.
Forgiving each other and forgiven,
My fellow messengers, a taciturn retinue,
Though they never stop busying themselves in their streets and
    marketplaces,
Simultaneously (as we are wont to say) here and there.

4
I wanted glory, fame, and power.
But not just in one city of modest renown.
So I fled to countries whose capitals
Had boulevards lustrous beneath incandescent lamps
And, here and there, the outlines of Ionic columns.
I did not learn to value the honors one received there.
A sandy plain showed through every form.
So I ran farther, to the center of Megalopolis
In the belief that there was a center, though there was none.
I would have wept over my exposed delusion
Had the custom of regretting our offenses been preserved.
At best I would prostrate myself
And turn to my silent retinue:
Tell me, why should it be me, why exactly me?
Where are the others whose love was real and strong?
Should he remain faithful who didn't want to be faithful?

5
I made a pledge, what kind, I don't remember.
I wore a silver scout badge, then a gold one.

I took an oath, in mystical lodges, in underground assemblies
Swearing by the freedom of the people, or perhaps by brotherhood.
I wasn't to be obedient to my slogans or my chiefs.
Some lazy earthly spirits from under the roots of trees
Had obviously made other arrangements
Having a little laugh at the expense of my morals.
Engaged in weighty discussion on killing for the common good
My clear-eyed companions glanced distractedly
As I passed their table, a naive lute player.
And while they sat at their chess games (the winner was to execute the
    verdict)
I believed they were taking part in the tournaments for fun.
How I envied them: so magnificent,
So free from what I guarded as my shameful secret:
That, like the mermaid from Andersen's tale
I tried to walk correctly but a thin pain
Reminded me that I was foolish to try to imitate people.

6
And there was a holiday in Megalopolis.
Streets were closed to traffic, people walked in a procession.
The statue of a god slowly moved along:
A phallus four stories high
Surrounded by a crowd of priests and priestesses
Who tossed about in a whirling dance.
A service was also being celebrated in Christian churches
Where the liturgy consisted of discussion
Under the guidance of a priest in Easter vestment
On whether we should believe in life after death,
Which the president then put to the vote.
So I betook myself to an evening party
In a glass house at the edge of a mountain,
Where, silent, they stood observing a landscape of the planet:
A sparkling plain of metal or salt,

Absinthe lands furrowed by erosions,
White observatories far away on the summit.
The sun was setting in cardinal crimson.

After shootings and bitterness and songs and lamentations
It is not I who is going to tear at bandages and break seals.

What if I was merely an ignorant child
And served the voices that spoke through me?

Who can tell what purpose is served by destinies
And whether to have lived on earth means little
Or much.

VI. The Accuser

You say a name, but it's not known to anyone.

Either because that man died or because
He was a celebrity on the banks of another river.

Chiaromonte

Miomandre

Petöfi

Mickiewicz

Young generations are not interested in what happened
Somewhere else, long ago.

And what about your teachers who repeated:
Ars longa, vita brevis?

Their laurel-crowned deceptions will soon be over.

Do you still say to yourself: *non omnis moriar?*

Oh yes, not all of me shall die, there will remain
An item in the fourteenth volume of an encyclopedia
Next to a hundred Millers and Mickey Mouse.

A traveler. Far away. And a low sun.
You sit in a ditch and to your bearded mouth
You raise a slice of bread cut off with a penknife.
And there, splendor. Parades. Carriages. Youth all in flowers.
A short while ago you were one of them. Now you are watching.
Your sons ride there and do not know you.

You don't like this subject. Fine. Let's change it then.
What about those medieval dialogues before daybreak.
My most gracious and honorable body,
I, your soul, you declaim, I command you:
It's time to get up, check the date.
There are many tasks to be done today.
Serve me a little longer, just a bit.
I don't know what is going on in your dark tunnels,
At what moment you'll deny and overthrow me,
On what day your cosmos will congeal and collapse.

And you hear in reply: a bone cracks,
Murky blood grumbles, accelerates its rhythm,
Pain answers close in sign language,
A megalithic gurgle, whisper, indictments.

Confess, you have hated your body,
Loving it with unrequited love. It has not fulfilled
Your high expectations. As if you were chained to
Some little animal in perpetual unrest,
Or worse, to a madman, and a Slavic one at that.

What beauty. What light. An echo.
You lean from the window of a train, behind the house of the
    signalman
Children wave their kerchiefs. Woods flow by. An echo.
Or she, in a long dress embroidered in gold,
Steps down and down the stairs, your beloved.

The so-called sights of the earth. But not many.
You started on a journey and are not sated.
Spring dances go on but there is no dancer.

In truth, perhaps you never took part in all that.
A spirit pure and scornfully indifferent,
You wanted to see, to taste, to feel, and nothing more.
For no human purpose. You were a passerby
Who makes use of hands and legs and eyes
As an astrophysicist uses shiny screens,
Aware that what he perceives has long since perished.
"Tender and faithful animals." How is one to live with them
If they run and strive, while those things are no more?

Do you remember your textbook of Church History?
Even the color of the page, the scent of the corridors.
Indeed, quite early you were a gnostic, a Marcionite,
A secret taster of Manichean poisons.
From our bright homeland cast down to the earth,
Prisoners delivered to the ruin of our flesh,
Unto the Archon of Darkness. His is the house and law.
And this dove, here, over Bouffalowa Street
Is his as you yourself are. Descend, fire.
A flash—and the fabric of the world is undone.

This sin and guilt. And to whom should you complain?
I know your microscopes, your many labors,

And your secrets and your life spent
In the service of self-will, not out of self-will.

One summer day, one summer day.
A little armchair adorned with a garland of peonies and jasmine.
Your short legs dangle. All applaud.
A choir of peasants sings a song.

Until you reach the crossroads. There will be two paths.
One difficult and down, another easy and up.
Take the difficult one, simple Johnny. Again two paths.
One difficult and up, another easy and down.
Go up and it will lead you to the castle.

The road weaves upward accompanied by a drum and a flute,
Round and round the bends, where the scent is more and more
        honeyed.
Plaited beehives, their straw shines like brass,
Sunflowers in rows, thyme.
And there, four turrets: facing east, west, north, and south.
When you enter the gate it's as if they were waiting for you.
Complete silence in a rose garden,
Around it, an expanse of green hills,
Of blue-green, up to the very clouds.

A pebble grates on the path. And presto! you fly as in dreams.
Black and white griffins on marble floors,
Parquetry of dim rooms. Yes, you were expected.
You don't have to say who you are. Everyone here knows and loves you.
Eyes meeting eyes, hands touching hands. What communion.
What timeless music of saved generations.

And whoever that man is, from Provence, judging by his dress,
His words, when he addresses beautiful ladies, old men, and youths,

Are yours as well, as if he and you had long been one:
"Behold the sword that separates Tristan and Iseult.
Revealed to us was the contradiction between life and truth.
In the forgetting of earthly years is our movement and peace.
In our prayer for the last day is our consolation."

There was no castle. You were simply listening to a record.
A needle, swaying lightly on a black frozen pond,
Led the voices of dead poets out into the sun.
Then you thought in disgust:

Bestiality

Bestialité

Bestialità

Who will free me
From everything that my age will bequeath?
From infinity plus. From infinity minus.
From a void lifting itself up to the stars?

Throats.
Choking.
Fingers sinking.
Into flesh.
Which in an instant will cease to live.
A naked heap.
Quivering.
Without sound.
Behind thick glass.

And what if that was you, that observer behind thick glass?

Well, it happened long ago, in Ecbatana.
In Edessa, if you prefer. Be it as it may, a chronicle

In which nothing is certain and no evidence
Against any of you. Or against you alone.

You all rushed to arrange your households.
To smash tablets. Cart them away. Blood
Was washed from the walls with soap, sand, and chlorine.

In a barber's chair somewhere in a southern city.
Summer heat, jingling, a tambourine.
And a pythoness on the sidewalk
Rocks her swarthy belly in a ring of onlookers.
While here they trim your gray hair and sideburns
O Emperor.
Franz Josef.
Nicholas.
Ego.

—Yet I have learned how to live with my grief.

—As if putting words together has been of help.

—Not true, there were others, grace and beauty,
I bowed to them, revered them,
I brought them my gifts.

—And all you do is repeat:
If only there were enough time.
If only there were enough time.

You would like to lead a gathering of people
To a ritual of purification through the columns of a temple.

A ritual of purification? Where? When? For whom?

VII. Bells in Winter

Once, when returning from far Transylvania
Through mountain forests, rocks, and Carpathian ridges,
Halting by a ford at the close of day
(My companions had sent me ahead to look
For passage), I let my horse graze
And out of the saddlebag took the Holy Scripture;
The light was so gracious, murmur of streams so sweet,
That reading Paul's epistles, and seeing the first star,
I was soon lulled into a profound sleep.

A young man in ornate Greek raiment
Touched my arm and I heard his voice:
"Your time, O mortals, hastens by like water,
I have descended and known its abyss.
It was I, whom cruel Paul chastised in Corinth
For having stolen my father's wife,
And by his order I was to be excluded
From the table at which we shared our meals.
Since then I have not been in gatherings of the saints,
And for many years I was led by the sinful love
Of a poor plaything given to temptation,
And so we doomed ourselves to eternal ruin.
But my Lord and my God, whom I knew not,
Tore me from the ashes with his lightning,
In his eyes your truths count for nothing,
His mercy saves all living flesh."

Awake under a huge starry sky,
Having received help unhoped for,
Absolved of care about our paltry life,
I wiped my eyes wet with tears.

No, I have never been to Transylvania.
I have never brought messages from there to my church.
But I could have.
This is an exercise in style.
The pluperfect tense
Of countries imperfective.

But what I am going to tell you now is not invented.
The narrow street, just opposite the university
Was called, in fact, Literary Lane.
On the corner, a bookstore; but not books, just sheaves of paper
Up to the very ceiling. Unbound, tied with string,
Print and handwriting, in Latin, Cyrillic script,
In Hebrew letters. From a hundred, three hundred years ago.
Now it seems to me like quite a fortune.
From this bookstore you could see a similar one
Facing it. And their owners
Were similar, too: faded beards
Long black caftans, red eyelids.
They hadn't changed since the day Napoleon passed through the town.
Nothing has changed here. The privilege of stones?
They always are, for that is the way they like it. Beyond the second store
You turn along a wall and pass a house
Where a poet, famous in our city,
Wrote a tale about a princess named Grażyna.
Next, a wooden gate studded with nails
As huge as fists. Under the vault, to the right,
Stairs smelling of oil paint, where I live.

Not that I myself chose Literary Lane.
It just happened, there was a room for rent,
Low-ceilinged, with a bay window, an oak bed,
Heated well that severe winter by a stove

That used to devour logs brought from the hallway
By the old servant woman, Lisabeth.

There is, it would seem, no reason
(For I have departed to a land more distant
Than one that can be reached by roads leading through woods and
    mountains)
To bring that room back here.

Yet I belong to those who believe in *apokatastasis*.
That word promises reverse movement,
Not the one that was set in *katastasis,*
And appears in the Acts 3, 21.

It means: restoration. So believed: St. Gregory of Nyssa,
Johannes Scotus Erigena, Ruysbroeck, and William Blake.

For me, therefore, everything has a double existence.
Both in time and when time shall be no more.

And so, one morning. In biting frost,
All is cold and gray. And in that sleepy haze
A span of air suffused with carmine light.
Banks of snow, roadways made slippery by sleighs
Grow rosy. As do wisps of smoke, puffs of vapor.
Bells jingle nearby, then farther away, shaggy horses
Covered with hoarfrost, every hair distinct.
And then the pealing of bells. At Saint John's
And the Bernardines', at Saint Casimir's
And the Cathedral, at the Missionaries'
And Saint George's, at the Dominicans'
And Saint Nicholas's, at Saint Jacob's.
Many many bells. As if the hands pulling the ropes
Were building a huge edifice over the city.

As long as I intone:
Memento etiam, Domine, famulorum famularumque tuarum
Qui nos praecesserunt.

Kurie pirma musu nuėjo.

What year is this? It's easy to remember.
This is the year when eucalyptus forests froze in our hills
And everyone could provide himself with free wood for his fireplace
In preparation for the rains and storms from the sea.

In the morning we were cutting logs with a chain saw.
And it is a strong, fierce dwarf, crackling and rushing in the smell of
    combustion.
Below, the bay, the playful sun,
And the towers of San Francisco seen through rusty fog.

And always the same consciousness unwilling to forgive.

Perhaps only my reverence will save me.

If not for it, I wouldn't dare pronounce the words of prophets:

"Whatever can be Created can be Annihilated; Forms cannot;
The Oak is cut down by the Ax, the Lamb falls by the Knife,
But their Forms Eternal Exist forever. Amen. Hallelujah!

"For God himself enters Death's Door always with those that enter
And lies down in the Grave with them, in Visions of Eternity
Till they awake and see Jesus and the Linen Clothes lying
That the Females had woven for them and the Gates of their Father's
    House."

And if the city, there below, was consumed by fire
Together with the cities of all the continents,

So that Lisabeth wrapped up in her cape could go to morn
  Mass.

I have thought for a long time about Lisabeth's life.
I could count the years. But I prefer not to.
What are years, if I see the snow and her shoes,
Funny, pointed, buttoned on the side,
And I am the same, though the pride of the flesh
Has its beginning and its end.

Pudgy angels are blowing their trumpets again.
And him, the stooped priest in his chasuble
I would compare today to a scarab
From the Egyptian division of the Louvre.
Our sister Lisabeth in the communion of saints—
Of witches ducked and broken on the wheel
Under the image of the cloud-enfolded Trinity
Until they confess that they turn into magpies at night;
Of wenches used for their masters' pleasure;
Of wives who received a letter of divorce;
Of mothers with a package under a prison wall—
Follows the letters with her black fingernail,
When the choirmaster, a sacrificer, a Levite
Ascending the stairs, sings: *Introibo ad altare Dei.*
Ad Deum qui laetificat juventutem meam.

Prie Dievo kurs linksmina mano jaunystė.

Mano jaunystė.
My youth.
As long as I perform the rite
And sway the censer and the smoke of my words
Rises here.

I would not say with my mouth of ashes that it was unjust.
For we lived under the Judgment, unaware.

Which Judgment began in the year one thousand seven hundred fifty-
    seven.

Though not for certain, perhaps in some other year.
It shall come to completion in the sixth millennium, or next Tuesday.
The demiurge's workshop will suddenly be stilled. Unimaginable
    silence.
And the form of every single grain will be restored in glory.
I was judged for my despair because I was unable to understand this.

Berkeley, 1973–1974

A MAGIC MOUNTAIN

I don't remember exactly when Budberg died, it was either two years
    ago or three.
The same with Chen. Whether last year or the one before.
Soon after our arrival, Budberg, gently pensive,
Said that in the beginning it is hard to get accustomed,
For here there is no spring or summer, no winter or fall.

"I kept dreaming of snow and birch forests.
Where so little changes you hardly notice how time goes by.
This is, you will see, a magic mountain."

Budberg: a familiar name in my childhood.
They were prominent in our region,
This Russian family, descendants of German Balts.
I read none of his works, too specialized.
And Chen, I have heard, was an exquisite poet,
Which I must take on faith, for he wrote in Chinese.

Sultry Octobers, cool Julys, trees blossom in February.
Here the nuptial flight of hummingbirds does not forecast spring.
Only the faithful maple sheds its leaves every year.
For no reason, its ancestors simply learned it that way.

I sensed Budberg was right and I rebelled.
So I won't have power, won't save the world?
Fame will pass me by, no tiara, no crown?
Did I then train myself, myself the Unique,
To compose stanzas for gulls and sea haze,
To listen to the foghorns blaring down below?
Until it passed. What passed? Life.
Now I am not ashamed of my defeat.
One murky island with its barking seals
Or a parched desert is enough
To make us say: yes, *oui, si.*

"Even asleep we partake in the becoming of the world."
Endurance comes only from enduring.
With a flick of the wrist I fashioned an invisible rope,
And climbed it and it held me.

What a procession! *Quelles délices!*
What caps and hooded gowns!
Most respected Professor Budberg,
Most distinguished Professor Chen,
Wrong Honorable Professor Milosz
Who wrote poems in some unheard-of tongue.
Who will count them anyway. And here sunlight.
So that the flames of their tall candles fade.
And how many generations of hummingbirds keep them company
As they walk on. Across the magic mountain.
And the fog from the ocean is cool, for once again it is July.

Berkeley, 1975

TEMPTATION

Under a starry sky I was taking a walk,
On a ridge overlooking neon cities,
With my companion, the spirit of desolation,
Who was running around and sermonizing,
Saying that I was not necessary, for if not I, then someone else
Would be walking here, trying to understand his age.
Had I died long ago nothing would have changed.
The same stars, cities, and countries
Would have been seen with other eyes.
The world and its labors would go on as they do.

For Christ's sake, get away from me.
You've tormented me enough, I said.
It's not up to me to judge the calling of men.
And my merits, if any, I won't know anyway.

Berkeley, 1975

SECRETARIES

I am no more than a secretary of the invisible thing
That is dictated to me and a few others.
Secretaries, mutually unknown, we walk the earth
Without much comprehension. Beginning a phrase in the middle
Or ending it with a comma. And how it all looks when completed
Is not up to us to inquire, we won't read it anyway.

Berkeley, 1975

AMAZEMENT

O what daybreak in the windows! Cannons salute.
The basket boat of Moses floats down the green Nile.
Standing immobile in the air, we fly over flowers:
Lovely carnations and tulips placed on long low tables.
Heard too are hunting horns exclaiming *hallali*.
Innumerable and boundless substances of the Earth:
Scent of thyme, hue of fir, white frost, dances of cranes.
And everything simultaneous. And probably eternal.
Unseen, unheard, yet it was.
Unexpressed by strings or tongues, yet it will be.
Raspberry ice cream, we melt in the sky.

Berkeley, 1975

IDEA

Afoot, on horseback, with bugles and baying hounds,
We looked down at last on the wilderness of the Idea,
Sulphur yellow like an aspen forest in late fall
(If the memory of a previous life does not deceive me),
Though it was not a wood, but a tangle of inorganic forms,
Chlorine vapor and mercury and iridescence of crystals.
I glanced at our company: bows, muskets,
A five-shot rifle, here and there a sling.
And the outfits! The latest fashions from the year one thousand
Or, for variety, top hats such as Kierkegaard,
The preacher, used to wear on his walks.
Not an imposing crew. Though, in fact, the Idea
Was dangerous to our kind no more, even in its lair.
To assault poor shepherds, farmhands, lumberjacks
Was its specialty, since it had changed its habits.
And the youngsters above all. Tormenting them with dreams
Of justice on earth and the Island of the Sun.

Berkeley, 1976

NOTES

ON THE NEED TO DRAW BOUNDARIES
Wretched and dishonest was the sea.

REASON TO WONDER
The ruler of what elements gave us song to praise birth?

ACCORDING TO HERACLITUS
The eternally living flame, the measure of all things, just as the measure of wealth is money.

LANDSCAPE
Unbounded forests flowing with the honey of wild bees.

LANGUAGE
Cosmos, i.e., pain raved in me with a diabolic tongue.

SUPPLICATION
From galactic silence protect us.

JUST IN CASE
When I curse Fate, it's not me, but the earth in me.

FROM THE STORE OF PYTHAGOREAN PRINCIPLES
Having left your native land, don't look back, the Erinyes are behind you.

HYPOTHESIS
If, she said, you wrote in Polish to punish yourself for your sins, you will be saved.

PORTRAIT
He locked himself in a tower, read ancient authors, fed birds on the terrace.

For only in this way could he forget about having to know himself.

CONSOLATION
Calm down. Both your sins and your good deeds will be lost in oblivion.

DO UT DES
He felt thankful, so he couldn't not believe in God.

THE PERFECT REPUBLIC
Right from early morning—the sun has barely made it through the dense maples—they walk contemplating the holy word: Is.

THE TEMPTER IN THE GARDEN
A still-looking branch, both cold and living.

HARMONY
Deprived. And why shouldn't you be deprived?
Those better than you were deprived.

STRONG OR WEAK POINT
You were always ready to fall to your knees!
Yes, I was always ready to fall to my knees.

WHAT ACCOMPANIES US
Mountain stream, footbridge with a rail
remembered down to the smallest burr on its bark.

THE WEST
On straw-yellow hills, over a cold blue sea,
black bushes of thorny oak.

INSCRIPTION TO BE PLACED OVER THE UNKNOWN GRAVE OF L.F.
What was doubt in you, lost, what was faith in you, triumphed.

EPITAPH
You who think of us: they lived only in delusion,
Know that we, the People of the Book, will never die.

MEMORY AND MEMORY
Not to know. Not to remember. With this one hope:
That beyond the River Lethe, there is memory, healed.

A GOD-FEARING MAN
So God heard my request after all, and allowed me to sin in his praise.

AIM IN LIFE
Oh to cover my shame with regal attire!

MEDICINE
If not for the revulsion at the smell of his skin,
I could think I was a good man.

LONGING
Not that I want to be a god or a hero.
Just to change into a tree, grow for ages, not hurt anyone.

MOUNTAINS
Wet grass to the knees, in the clearing, raspberry bushes taller than a
man, a cloud on the slope, in the cloud a black forest. And shepherds in
medieval buskins were coming down as we walked up.

IN REVERSE
On the ruins of their homes grows a young forest. Wolves are returning
and a bear sleeps secure in a raspberry thicket.

MORNING
We awoke from a sleep of I don't know how many thousand years.
An eagle flew in the sun again but it didn't mean the same.

ABUNDANT CATCH (LUKE 5.4–10)

On the shore fish toss in the stretched nets of Simon, James, and John.
High above, swallows. Wings of butterflies. Cathedrals.

HISTORY OF THE CHURCH

For two thousand years I have been trying to understand what It was.

Berkeley, 1978

THE SEPARATE NOTEBOOKS

A Mirrored Gallery

(Page 1)
An old man, contemptuous, black-hearted,
Amazed that he was twenty such a short time ago,
Speaks.
    Though he would rather understand than speak.

He loved and desired, but it turned out badly.
He pursued and almost captured, but the world was faster than he was.
And now he sees the illusion.

In his dreams he is running through a dark garden.
His grandfather is there but the pear tree is not where it should be,
And the little gate opens to a breaking wave.

Inexorable earth.
Irrevocable law.
The light unyielding.

Now he climbs marble stairs
And the blossoming orange trees are fragrant
And he hears, for a while, the *tiuu* of birds,
But the heavy doors are already closing
Behind which he will stay for a very long time
In air that does not know winter or spring,
In a fluorescence without mornings and without sunsets.

The coffers of the ceiling imitate a forest vault.
He passes through halls full of mirrors
And the faces loom up and dissolve,
Just as Barbara, the princess, appeared to the king once
When a black mage had conjured her.
And all around him the voices are intoning,

So many that he could listen for centuries,
Because he wanted, once, to understand his poor life.

(Page 10)
Sacramento River, among barren hills, tawny,
And spurts of shallow wind from the bay
And on the bridges my tires drum out a meter.

Ships, black animals among the islands,
Gray winter on the waters and the sky.
If they could be called in from their far-off Aprils and countries,
Would I know how to tell them what is worst yet true—
The wisdom, not for them, that has come to me?

(Page 12)
He found on dusty shelves the pages of a family chronicle covered with
barely legible writing, and again he visits the murky house on the Dvina
where he had been once in his childhood, called The Castle because it
had been built where, at the time of Napoleon, a castle of the Knights
of the Sword had burned down, exposing dungeons in the foundations
and a skeleton chained to the wall. It was also called The Palace, to dis-
tinguish it from the cottage in the park where Eugene used to move,
together with his piano, for the winter. That relative of his had gone
to Jesuit schools in Metz and made a career as a lawyer in the mili-
tary courts of St. Petersburg, but left the service when he was asked
to convert to Orthodoxy; after which he returned to The Castle and
lived alone, maintaining relations with none of the neighbors nor with
his family, except his sister Mrs. Jadwiga Iżycka, whom he loved. *"They
conversed with the servants only in Polish or Byelorussian, holding the Russian
language in abomination."* With rare guests, former colleagues from St.
Petersburg, Eugene spoke French. *"He remained in The Castle, practically
without leaving it, from 1893 to 1908. He used to read a great deal, also to
write, but mostly, night and day, he played the piano. It was a cabinet model, a
Korngoff of Warsaw make, for which he paid 1500 rubles in gold, in those times*

an enormous sum." If he went anywhere, it was on horseback to visit his sister at the neighboring Idolta, and they were often seen riding together through the forests, for she was fond of riding on an "amazon" saddle. But after her death, only a passerby, stopping at the park's gate and hearing his exquisite music, could have testified that the house was inhabited. Later on, no music was heard, *"though it was already autumn, and so people assumed that he still played, but in the far interior of The Palace where, because of the double windows, he could not be heard."* Then, suddenly, he convoked the family and even admitted priests. He was buried beside his sister in the family vault at Idolta. He left behind packages of manuscripts, of unknown contents, bound with string.

(Page 13)
I did not choose California. It was given to me.
What can the wet north say to this scorched emptiness?
Grayish clay, dried-up creek beds,
Hills the color of straw, and the rocks assembled
Like Jurassic reptiles: for me this is
The spirit of the place.
And the fog from the ocean creeping over it all,
Incubating the green in the arroyos
And the prickly oak and the thistles.

Where is it written that we deserve the earth for a bride,
That we plunge in her deep, clear waters
And swim, carried by generous currents?

(Page 14)
He reads in the chronicle: *"Soon after his death, he began to frighten people. From that time there was no peace in The Castle, for everybody would say that Pan Eugene was walking. Furniture moved, the desk in his room changed place, the piano played at night in his study, and there were weird goings-on in the library upstairs."* This unpleasant discovery was made by an agent of the Bank of Wilno, Mr. Mieczysław Jałowiecki, who was assessing the estate

in connection with the heirs' endeavors to get a loan. They made a bed for him in Eugene's study, a large room with an oak parquet floor and windows facing the Dvina, where beside a piano and a desk there were bookcases for those books which Eugene wanted to have at hand without having to walk upstairs to the library; and one's attention was drawn by paintings and a valuable clock from the time of the Directorate, adorned with Napoleonic eagles. In the middle of the night the guest, ringing—in horror—the bell for the servants, tore off the thick woolen bell pull and, without waiting for rescue, jumped out of the window in his underwear, for which rashness he paid with pneumonia, since it was cold outside. Eventually everyone became accustomed to troubles in The Castle, but what happened to the new parish priest in Druja, Canon Father Weber, was unusual. He came to The Castle to pay a visit, and looking casually through albums of photographs suddenly stopped at one of them and asked whom it represented. When he heard from his hostess that the figure was her brother-in-law Eugene who had died two years before, he said, *"Strange, I don't know if I should mention it, Madam—perhaps it would be better not, for you may think I have lost my mind, saying such things—yet, whether you believe me or not, I must tell you that he was in my room at the monastery yesterday night."* And he told how, after having returned from an inspection of his parish, he went to bed early, and began to read to induce sleep, when he heard the door creaking, steps in the dining room and then in the living room which adjoined his chamber. The door opened and an unknown man entered, elegantly dressed, *"with the energetic bearing of a man of wealth, full of self-assurance,"* bareheaded and without an overcoat. Father Weber took him for one of the neighboring landlords whom he had not as yet met, arriving on some urgent business, and he began to excuse himself for being found so early in bed. The unknown man approached him silently, rested his hand on the marble top of the night table, and said, *"As proof that I was here, I leave my fingerprints."* And then he turned and left. Without hurry, he crossed the unlit living room, then the dining room, opened the door to the corridor of the former monastery, and gradually his steps fell silent. Yet, as the priest was later able to assure himself, the door leading to the yard was locked, as was the gate to the street and the wicket in the gate. Eugene continued to remind people of himself until precisely that day in February 1914 when his brother Józef passed away. I wonder, thinks the reader, whether philosophy is really of any help against the passion of life? Perhaps all of wisdom is good for nothing if petty angers and ill feelings and family quarrels are so durable that they force us to walk after our death?

(Page 15)

> Le Monde—*c'est terrible*
>
> —CÉZANNE

Cézanne, I bring these three for an impossible meeting
to your workshop in Aix, into the fire of ocher and cinnabar.

This woman's name is Gabriela. I could show her
in a white dress with a sailor's collar
or as an old hag with protruding, gumless teeth.
Here she stands olive-gold, black-haired.

This is Eddy, an athlete from half a century ago.
He rests his hand on his hip as in the portrait
reproduced sometimes in art books.

And here is Mieczystaw who painted him. Fingers yellow from tobacco,
he licks a cigarette paper, thinking about the next move of his brush.

They will be witnesses to my grief,
and to whom should I reveal it, if not to you?

Strength, skill, beauty, above all strength,
swinging one's shoulders, an easy gait
are what people value most highly, and justly so.
A movement in harmony with the universal movement, deftness,
whatever the world is, makes one happy.

To be like him when he bends into the crouch of a discus thrower,
when he urges his horse into a gallop, slips at dawn from the window
of the redhaired wife of Mr. Z!

I envied him as only a sixteen-year-old can do.
Until, not soon, after the big war,
news of him reached me. He had not perished in battle.
In a new State, under the rule of a debased language,
he poisoned himself with gas out of loathing for the everyday lie.

If glory of flesh falls into the earth,
into the general oblivion. If I, the mind,
have such power over him that at my order
he appears, though he is no one until the end of the world,
have I triumphed? Is not that a miserable revenge?

Whatever was desired, Cézanne,
was changing like the trunk of a Provençal pine when you tilted your
      head.
The color of her dress and skin: the yellow, the rouge,
the sienna raw and burnt, the green Veronese,
words like tubes of color ready-made and alien.
And Gabriela remains only that.

I want to know where it goes, that moment of enchantment,
to what heaven above, to the bottom of what abyss,
to what gardens growing beyond space and time.
I want to know where the house of an instant of seeing is,
when it's liberated from the eye, in itself forever,
the one you pursued day after day
circling a tree with your easels.

Mieczysław had his workshop in the city of Warsaw.
Your tardy disciple, he nearly achieved,

as he used to tell me, blowing on his cold fingers
that war winter, a clay jar and an apple.
He looked at them constantly and constantly they filled his canvases.

And I believe he would have snatched from things a moment of seeing,
had he observed the rules of the artist
who must be indifferent to good and evil,
to joy and pain and the laments of mortals,
a haughty servant, as he is, of only one aim.

But he used his workshop to help people
and hid Jews there, for which the penalty was death.
He was executed in May 1943,
thus giving his soul for his friends.

And it is bitter to sing in praise of the mind, Cézanne.

The three names are real and because of that they exert control. Had they
been changed, the road to fictionalizing would, immediately, have been
opened. Yet the more he tries to be precise, the more entangled he gets
in devices of human speech. And it is enough to put those three, quite
arbitrarily, together, and suddenly what is untellable in them is strength-
ened, composing itself into an autonomous tale. But yes, also in reality
they stood together once, in a photo, not alone, with others, before the
house in Krasnogruda, and each one of them lived in the thoughts of his
neighbor. He tries now to guess how he thinks of them. Eddy is a panic
of remembered shames: not saving a goal, kicking down the jumping
bar, falling from a horse, things which should not be known by anybody.
When he learned that Eddy married shortly before the war, that he and
his wife were inseparable, that they survived those years together and, by
mutual consent, committed suicide in 1951 or 1952, he felt, yes, relief, as
if the disappearance of a man compared to whom he felt himself infe-
rior elevated him. As for Gabriela, her presence is nearly as intense as
that of the river on whose banks he was born and where he, three years

old, saw her, a teenager, for the first time. A golden net on ultramarine, or green, green Veronese, an acrid sweetness of honeycombs brought in in a clay bowl, a neck like the necks of musical instruments—she was never expected to be all this for him, constantly rescued, taken out of time. And about Mieczysław he thinks that even if a life was refused to him in which he could win as an artist and all his paintings were burned except for the portrait of Eddy which he painted in his youth, at least he was happy once, arranging an apartment with Julia in the quarter of modern buildings or wandering with her in the Gorce mountains at the end of the nineteen twenties, when Warsaw artists and literati loved mountaineering lore, naive paintings on glass, and folk songs. He does not know why, but there is some consolation in that, just as there is in the little song Mieczysław hummed, sometimes, with a kind of embarrassed emotion:

> "Round and round
> The little sun is going
> The little sun is going
> And our Catherine
> Is riding to her wedding
> Is riding to her wedding
> Is riding, is riding
> And lifting her hands
> And lifting her hands
> Asking Jesus
> Asking Jesus
> To make her happy."

He thinks that the word *past* does not mean anything, for if he can keep those three so strongly before his eyes, how much stronger than his is an unearthly gaze.

(Page 17)

A portrait of Schopenhauer consorts, who knows why, with a portrait of Ela who, adorned by the painter with a Renaissance hat similar, probably, to those worn by ladies on the deck of the *Titanic,* smiles enigmatically. "Ah, philosopher," the wanderer addresses him, "I have found out why they dislike you. Who, after all, wants to be told that truth is a rebellion of the mind against its utilitarian vocation? That fate is aristocratic in allocating the gifts of intellect, and that they, completely average, chasing illusion, are supposed to bow to the fewest of the few and admit their own inferiority? *'He is rather like a theatergoer, for separated from everything he watches the drama.'* One in how many millions, the artist and philosopher? And myself too, had I known in advance what was in store for me, wouldn't I have chosen life and happiness? Even now, when I know that what remains of the life and happiness of my contemporaries is nothing? It is easy to guess why you were not liked and never will be. No one had ever so forcefully opposed the child and the genius to the rest of them, always under the power of blind will, of which the essence is sexual desire; no one has ever so forcefully explained the genius of children: they are onlookers, avid, gluttonous, minds not yet caught by the will of the species, though I would add, led too by Eros, but an Eros who is still free and dances, knowing nothing of goals and service. And the gift of the artist or philosopher likewise has its secret in a hidden hostility toward the earth of the adults. Your language—O philosopher—so logical and precise in its appearance, disguised more than it revealed, so they really had no access to you. Admit it, your only theme was time: a masque on midsummer night, young girls in bloom, ephemerid generations born and dying in a single hour. You asked only one question—is it worthy of man to be seduced and caught?"

(Page 18)
Lovers walk in the morning on a path above the village, they look down into the valley, dazzled by themselves and by their part in the earth of the living.

Brookwater below, green meadows, and on the opposite slope the forest tiers up steeply.

They go where a black woodpecker flickers among the firs and the scent of new clover rises from the edge of the gorge.

And now they have found a footbridge among the trees, a true bridge with a handrail, that leads somewhere, on the other side.

And when they walk down, they see in a frame of pines the roofs of two towers, green copper glistening, and they hear the thin voice of a little bell.

That cloister, small cars high above it on the road, and, in the sun, the echo and then silence.

As the beginning of a revelation—what kind they don't know—because it will never advance beyond its beginning.

"Philosopher, you were too severe for their short-lived élans of the ego, though even then they looked at things as if the vainglory of existence were in the past. And I concede, your words confirmed what I had experienced myself: '. . . the quiet contemplation of the natural object actually present, whether a landscape, a tree, a mountain, a building or whatever it may be; in as much as he loses himself in this object, i.e., forgets even his individuality, his will, and only continues to exist as the pure subject, the clear mirror of the object, so that it is as if the object alone were there, without anyone to perceive it, and he can no longer separate the perceiver from the perception but both have become one, because the whole consciousness is filled and occupied with one single sensuous picture; if thus the object has to such an extent passed out of all relation to the will, then that which is so known is no longer the particular thing as such; but it is the Idea, the eternal form, the immediate objectivity of the will at this grade; and, therefore, he who is sunk in this perception is no longer individual, for in such perception the individual has lost himself; but he is the pure, will-less, powerless, timeless subject of knowledge.' "

(Page 20)

The earth in its nakedness of hard lava carved by river beds, the vast earth, void, from before the vegetation.

And the river they came to, called by adventurers Columbia, rolls down her waters, a cold and liquid lava as gray as if there were neither sky nor white clouds above.

Nothing here, except the winds of the planet raising dust from the eroded rock.

And, after a hundred miles, they reach the building on the plateau, and when they enter it, an old dream of a volcanic desert comes true;

For this is a museum, preserving the embroideries of princesses, the cradle of a crown prince, photographs of the cousins and nieces of a forgotten dynasty.

The wind beats loudly against the brass door, while the parquets squeak under the portraits of Czar Nicholas and of the Romanian queen, Maria.

What madman chose this place to dispose the souvenirs of his adoration, lilac-colored scarves and dresses in crêpe de chine?

For the eternal bitterness of the lost fleshliness of lovely girls traveling with their families to Biarritz.

For the degradation of touches and whispers by the mutterings of strewn pumice and basalt gravel.

Until even regret wears thin, and a deaf-dumb abstract ache remains?

His name was Sam Hill and he was a millionaire. On the windy heights where the Columbia River, flowing down out of the Rocky Mountains, had carved canyons for itself in volcanic layers from the time of the Pliocene, and where, a little later, men traced a border between central Washington and central Oregon, he started to build an edifice in 1914 which was to serve as a museum honoring his friend Maria of Romania. A beauty on the throne, eldest daughter of the Duke of Edinburgh and Saxe-Coburg-Gotha and of the Great Princess of Russia, Mary, thus cousin to both King George and Czar Nicholas II, she was eighteen when, in 1893, she married Prince Ferdinand Hohenzollern-Sigmaringen, the Romanian Crown Prince. It was rumored that she had *une cuisse légère,* i.e., a light thigh. Whatever the truth was, Sam Hill named his building Maryhill, uniting her name to his, and the inauguration of the museum in 1926 took place with the active participation of the royal guest. The few tourists who wander that way are able to take a look at her in Romanian folk dress; also to marvel at her sculptured throne, her spinning wheel, and her loom. Her toilets are preserved in the showcases, the walls adorned with portraits of her relatives, predominantly the Czar's family.

(Page 24)
If not now, when?
Here is the Phoenix airfield,
I see the cones of volcanic mountains
And I think of all I have not said,
About the words to *suffer* and *sufferance* and how one can bear a lot
By training anger until it gets tired and gives up.
Here is the island Kauai, an emerald set among white clouds,
Warm wind in the palm leaves, and I think of snow
In my distant province where things happened
That belong to another, inconceivable life.
The bright side of the planet moves toward darkness
And the cities are falling asleep, each in its hour,
And for me, now as then, it is too much.
There is too much world.

Waiting indefinitely. Every day and in every hour, hungry. A spasm in the throat, staring at the face of every woman passing in the street. Wanting not her but all the earth. Inhaling, with dilated nostrils, the smells of the bakery, of roasting coffee, wet vegetables. In thought devouring every dish and drinking every drink. Preparing myself for absolute possession.

(Page 25)
You talked, but after your talking all the rest remains.
After your talking—poets, philosophers, contrivers of romances—
Everything else, all the rest deduced inside the flesh
Which lives and knows, not just what is permitted.

I am a woman held fast now in a great silence.
Not all creatures have your need for words.
Birds you killed, fish you tossed into your boat,
In what words will they find rest and in what Heaven?

You received gifts from me; they were accepted.
But you don't understand how to think about the dead.
The scent of winter apples, of hoarfrost, and of linen:
There are nothing but gifts on this poor, poor earth.

A dark Academy. Assembled are instructresses in corsets, grammarians of petticoats, poets of unmentionables with lace. The curriculum includes feeling the touch of silk against the skin, listening to the rustle of a dress, raising the chin when the aigrette on the hat sways. They teach the use of what is customary: long gloves up to the elbows, a fan, lowered eyelashes, bows, as well as human speech, so that a faience chamberpot, even if a painted eye looks up roguishly from the bottom, is called a *vessel,* a brassiere lifting the breasts bears the name *soutiengorge,* and, in the spirit of French great-grandmothers who remembered the red coats of English soldiers, a menstruation is announced as *"the English have arrived."* The superior method and goal lies in a hardly noticeable smile, for everything is only make-believe: sounds of orchestras and promenades, paintings in gilded frames, hymns, chorals, marble sculptures, speeches of statesmen, and the words of chronicles. In reality there is only a sensation of warmth and gluiness inside, also a sober watchfulness when one advances to meet that delicious and dangerous thing that has no name, though people call it *life*.

(Page 27)
How many before me crossed over the frontier of words
Knowing the futility of speech after a century of phantoms
Which were terrifying but meant nothing?

What am I to do with the conductor of the Trans-Siberian Railway,
With the lady to whom a traveler offered a ring from Mongolia,
With singing expanses of telephone wires
And lush coupés and a station after the third bell?

They are all standing in front of the porch, dressed in white,
And through sooty pieces of glass they look at the eclipse
In the summer of 1914 in the Kowno gubernia.
And I am there, not knowing how or what will happen.
But they do not know either how or what will happen,
Or that this boy, now one of them,
Will wander as far as a precipice across the frontier of words,
Once, at the end of his life, when they will be no more.

(Page 29)
In the shadow of the Empire, in Old Slavonic long-johns,
You better learn to like your shame because it will stay with you.
It won't go away even if you change your country and your name.
The dolorous shame of failure. Shame of the muttony heart.
Of fawning eagerness. Of clever pretending.
Of dusty roads on the plain and trees lopped off for fuel.
You sit in a shabby house, putting things off until spring.
No flowers in the garden—they would be trampled anyway.

You eat lazy pancakes, the soupy dessert called "Nothing-served-cold."
And, always humiliated, you hate foreigners.

(Page 31)
Pure beauty, benediction: you are all I gathered
From a life that was bitter and confused,
In which I learned about evil, my own and not my own.
Wonder kept seizing me, and I recall only wonder,
Risings of the sun over endless green, a universe
Of grasses, and flowers opening to the first light,
Blue outline of the mountain and a hosanna shout.
I asked, how many times, is this the truth of the earth?
How can laments and curses be turned into hymns?
What makes you need to pretend, when you know better?
But the lips praised on their own, on their own the feet ran;
The heart beat strongly; and the tongue proclaimed its adoration.

(Page 34)
And why all this ardor if death is so close?
Do you expect to hear and see and feel there?
But you know the earth is like no other place:
What continents, what oceans, what a show it is!
In the hall of pain, what abundance on the table.
The music endures, but not the music-maker:
No velvet of his survives, not even a garter.
And space-age men, in thickets, lift bows to fiddles,
Drink in their villages, squabble, let dice rattle
Perched with the dead on a giddy carousel.

I have lived a life that makes me feel unable
To bring myself to write an accusation.
Joy would spurt in amid the lamentation.
So what, if, in a minute I must close the book:
Life's sweet, but it might be pleasant not to have to look.

THE SEPARATE NOTEBOOKS

The Wormwood Star

(Page 38)
Now there is nothing to lose, my cautious, my cunning, my hyperselfish cat.

Now we can make confession, without fear that it will be used by mighty enemies.

We are an echo that runs, skittering, through a train of rooms.

Seasons flare and fade, but as in a garden we do not enter anymore.

And that's a relief, for we do not need to catch up with the others, in the sprints and the high jump.

The Earth has not been to Your Majesty's liking.

The night a child is conceived, an obscure pact is concluded.

And the innocent receives a sentence, but he won't be able to unravel its meaning.

Even if he consults ashes, stars, and flights of birds.

A hideous pact, an entanglement in blood, an anabasis of vengeful genes arriving from swampy millennia,

From the half-witted and the crippled, from crazed wenches and syphilitic kings

At mutton's leg and barley and the slurping of soup.

Baptized with oil and water when the Wormwood Star was rising,

I played in a meadow by the tents of the Red Cross.

That was the time assigned to me, as if a personal fate were not enough.

In a small archaic town ("The bell on the City Hall clock chimed midnight, as a student N . . ." and so on).

How to speak? How to tear apart the skin of words?
What I have written seems to me now not that.
And what I have lived seems to me now not that.

When Thomas brought the news that the house I was born in no longer exists,

Neither the lane nor the park sloping to the river, nothing,

I had a dream of return. Multicolored. Joyous. I was able to fly.

And the trees were even higher than in childhood, because they had been growing during all the years since they had been cut down.

The loss of a native province, of a homeland,

Wandering one's whole life among foreign tribes—

Even this

Is only romantic, i.e., bearable.

Besides, that's how my prayer of a high school student was answered, of a boy who read the bards and asked for greatness which means exile.

The Earth has not been to Your Majesty's liking,

For a reason having nothing to do with the Planetary State.

Nonetheless I am amazed to have reached a venerable age.

And certainly I have experienced miraculous narrow escapes for which I vowed to God my gratitude,

So the horror of those days visited me as well.

(Page 39)
He hears voices but he does not understand the screams, prayers, blasphemies, hymns which chose him for their medium. He would like to know who he was, but he does not know. He would like to be one, but he is a self-contradictory multitude which gives him some joy, but more shame. He remembers tents of the Red Cross on the shore of a lake at a place called Wyshki. He remembers water scooped out of the boat, big gray waves and a bulb-like Orthodox church which seems to emerge from them. He thinks of that year, 1916, and of his beautiful cousin Ela in the uniform of an army nurse, of her riding through hundreds of versts along the front with a handsome officer, whom she has just married. Mama, covered with a shawl, is sitting by the fireplace at dusk with Mr. Niekrasz whom she knows from her student days at Riga, and his epaulets glitter. He had disturbed their conversation, but now he sits quietly and looks intently at the bluish flames, for she has told him that if he looks long enough he will see a funny little man with a pipe in there, riding around.

(Page 40)
What should we do with the child of a woman? ask the Powers
Above the Earth. The barrel of a cannon
Leaps, recoiling. Again. And a plain flares up
As far as the horizon. Thousands of them, running.

In the park on the lake shore tents of the Red Cross
Among hedges, flower beds, vegetable gardens.
Now, into a gallop: the nurse's veil, streaming.
A pitch-black stallion rearing; stubble, ravines.
At the river bank, red-bearded soldiers rowing.
Opens, through the smoke, a forest of broken firs.

(Page 41)
Our knowledge is not profound, say the Powers.
We come to know their pain but without compassion.
We wonder at the radiance under the clouds,
At the humility of the Mother, Substance, the Earth, a virgin.
Why should we care about living and dying?

(Page 42)
On all fours they crawled out of the dugout. Dawn.
Far away, under a cold aurora, an armored train.

(Page 43)
He walks, not like the soldier in the song, worn and weary, through the
fields and forest dreary, but through many rooms in which the sounds
and colors of forms that have come into being crackle, glitter, and boil
up. Here a band of bagpipers sequestered in a medieval village climbs a
grassy slope toward a plateau where they are going to play to the battle;
there the flood waters of the river Wilia have risen so high that they reach
the steps of the cathedral, and, under the sharp light of April, rowboats
painted with blue, white, and green stripes cruise around under the cathe-
dral tower; over there, little boys gathering raspberries have stumbled on
a cemetery overgrown with hopbines and bend down to decipher names:
Faust, Hildebrand. Indeed, why should we care about living and dying?

(Page 44)
Ladies of 1920 who served us cocoa.
Grow strong for the glory of Poland, our little knights, our eagles!

"Jackets carmine, buttons bright." And the lancers enter the city gate.
Ladies from the Polish Circle, ladies from the Auxiliary Corps.

(Page 45)
To the museum I carted frock-coats laced with silver,
Snuffboxes of speakers from chambers of deputies.
The hooves of draft horses clattered on the asphalt,
In the empty streets the smell of putrefaction.
We kept guzzling vodka, we drivers.

(Page 46)
"Mère des souvenirs, maîtresse des maîtresses." Vlad drove him from the bus
station in a carriage called a *dokart,* and nobody there knew or cared that
the name meant "dogcart." A road through a windy, treeless upland, full of
potholes and not much traveled. Below to the right, a middle-sized lake,
farther on, an isthmus: on one side, an eye of water among green fields;
on the other, a large shimmering expanse set among hills of juniper and
postdiluvian rock. The white spot of a grebe in the middle of that scal-
ing brightness. They turned left onto a dirt road from which one more
lake was visible, passed through a village in a dell at its end, and turned
up through a forest of pine, fir, and hazel scrub, which meant they were
practically home.

"—Who is going to reproach me for lack of precision, who would
recognize the places or the people? My power is absolute, everything there
belongs to one man now, who once, a student from Wilno, arrived there
in a dogcart. I decide whether or not I want to tell, for instance, who
Vlad was, that before World War I he studied engineering in Karlsruhe;
or who Aunt Florentyna was, that in the time of her youth an old for-
est still formed a huge natural wall on the three kilometers of holms and
slopes between this and the other, immense lake, and that it was she who
used to buy those French novels in yellow covers: Bourget, Gyp, Daudet.
What to select, what to leave out depends on my will, and I wonder at my
reluctance to indulge in fiction, as if I believed that one could faithfully
reconstruct what once was. And why Florentyna? It is hard to take in: that

I am allowed now to address her informally, though then I would not have dared, and that she is not an old lady but simultaneously a young girl and a child and all of them. What do I have to do with her, in her corsets and bustle skirts, unimaginable in her physical needs, taking her daughters to Warsaw, Paris, Venice, and Biarritz? And yet it was precisely my reflecting on her that introduced me to the kingdom of the purely empirical. How she had to make do: instead of having a manager and servants, her daughters get up at dawn—kneeboots, sheepskin coats—go to the stable, to the pigsty, assign work to farmhands, in winter supervise the threshing until evening. And for three months every year, there is no manor, just a boardinghouse for paying guests; in Kathleen's kitchen a fire burns from four in the morning until late at night, Vlad pounds on the piano for hours, and they, those guests, dance. She had also to accept a tacit change in customs; she had to decide not to notice whether her daughters had men with the blessing of marriage or without, so that, besides Vlad, someone else would live on the premises, George or some other boy. Everything was as it was, unspoken, so that an inevitable dailiness turned the strictest principles into those human inventions which evaporate without anyone bothering to say yes or no. There were no trips to church, except sometimes for Florentyna's sake. And she, with her two not-too-Catholic daughters, became my hidden thought about the sheer relativity of beliefs and convictions, which cannot resist the law of things."

And really, for him, spinning this monologue, why shouldn't what he learned there be enough? He had thought that he found himself there by chance and for the time being, that it was just a preface to something, but later on, too, there was nothing more than a preface and for the time being.

(Page 47)
For some hundred years that fabric, fleecy,
Thick as felt, was used to manufacture robes,
So you can't tell whether it is the end or the beginning of the twentieth
    century,
Now, when she, sitting before her mirror, opens the folds of her gown,

Bright yellow on the rose bronze of her breasts.
Nor has the brush in her hand changed its shape.
And the window frame belongs to any time,
And the view onto ash trees bent by the wind.
And who is she, in this one flesh only,
Inhabiting this one moment?
By whom is she to be seen
If she is deprived even of her name?
Her skin in the third person is for nobody,
Her most smooth skin in the third person does not exist.
And look—from behind the trees clouds rush in
Bordered with coppery lace, and all this
Stalls, hardens, and rises into light.

(Page 48)
Northern sunset, beyond the lake a song of harvesters.
They move about, tiny, binding the last sheaves.
Who has the right to imagine how they return to the village,
And sit down by the fire and cook and cut their bread?
Or how their fathers lived in huts without chimneys,
When every roof would smoke as if on fire?
Or how the land was once, before being given to the winds,
Quiet, the lakes like eyes in the untouched forest?
And who has the right to guess how the sun will set in the future
Over a prison train or the sleep of rigs on building sites,
To make himself a god who looks into their windows
And shakes his head and walks off full of pity because he knows so much?
You, my young hunter, had better just ease your canoe from the shore
And pick up the killed mallard before it gets dark.

(Page 49)
In a night train, completely empty, clattering through fields and woods,
a young man, my ancient self, incomprehensibly identical with me, tucks

up his legs on a hard bench—it is cold in the wagon—and in his slumber hears the clap of level crossings, echo of bridges, thrum of spans, the whistle of the locomotive. He wakes up, rubs his eyes, and above the tossed-back scarecrows of the pines he sees a dark-blue expanse in which, low on the horizon, one blood-red star is glowing.

(Page 50)

THE WORMWOOD STAR
Under the Wormwood Star bitter rivers flowed.
Man in the fields gathered bitter bread.
No sign of divine care shone in the heavens.
The century wanted homage from the dead.

They traced their origin to the dinosaur
And took their deftness from the lemur's paw.
Above the cities of the thinking lichen,
Flights of pterodactyls proclaimed the law.

They tied the hands of man with barbed wire.
And dug shallow graves at the edge of the wood.
There would be no truth in his last testament.
They wanted him anonymous for good.

The planetary empire was at hand.
They said what was speech and what was listening.
The ash had hardly cooled after the great fire
When Diocletian's Rome again stood glistening.

Berkeley, 1977–1978

BYPASSING RUE DESCARTES

Bypassing rue Descartes
I descended toward the Seine, shy, a traveler,
A young barbarian just come to the capital of the world.

We were many, from Jassy and Koloshvar, Wilno and Bucharest, Saigon
    and Marrakesh,
Ashamed to remember the customs of our homes,
About which nobody here should ever be told:
The clapping for servants, barefooted girls hurry in,
Dividing food with incantations,
Choral prayers recited by master and household together.

I had left the cloudy provinces behind,
I entered the universal, dazzled and desiring.

Soon enough, many from Jassy and Koloshvar, or Saigon or Marrakesh
Would be killed because they wanted to abolish the customs of their
    homes.

Soon enough, their peers were seizing power
In order to kill in the name of the universal, beautiful ideas.

Meanwhile the city behaved in accordance with its nature,
Rustling with throaty laughter in the dark,
Baking long breads and pouring wine into clay pitchers,
Buying fish, lemons, and garlic at street markets,
Indifferent as it was to honor and shame and greatness and glory,
Because that had been done already and had transformed itself
Into monuments representing nobody knows whom,
Into arias hardly audible and into turns of speech.

Again I lean on the rough granite of the embankment,
As if I had returned from travels through the underworlds

And suddenly saw in the light the reeling wheel of the seasons
Where empires have fallen and those once living are now dead.

There is no capital of the world, neither here nor anywhere else,
And the abolished customs are restored to their small fame
And now I know that the time of human generations is not like the
    time of the earth.

As to my heavy sins, I remember one most vividly:
How, one day, walking on a forest path along a stream,
I pushed a rock down onto a water snake coiled in the grass.

And what I have met with in life was the just punishment
Which reaches, sooner or later, the breaker of a taboo.

Berkeley, 1980

RIVERS

Under various names, I have praised only you, rivers!

You are milk and honey and love and death and dance.

From a spring in hidden grottoes, seeping from mossy rocks

Where a goddess pours live water from a pitcher,

At clear streams in the meadow, where rills murmur underground,

Your race and my race begin, and amazement, and quick passage.

Naked, I exposed my face to the sun, steering with hardly a dip of the
    paddle—

Oak woods, fields, a pine forest skimming by,

Around every bend the promise of the earth,

Village smoke, sleepy herds, flights of martins over sandy bluffs.

I entered your waters slowly, step by step,

And the current in that silence took me by the knees

Until I surrendered and it carried me and I swam

Through the huge reflected sky of a triumphant noon.

I was on your banks at the onset of midsummer night

When the full moon rolls out and lips touch in the rituals of kissing—

I hear in myself, now as then, the lapping of water by the boathouse

And the whisper that calls me in for an embrace and for consolation.

We go down with the bells ringing in all the sunken cities.

Forgotten, we are greeted by the embassies of the dead,

While your endless flowing carries us on and on;

And neither is nor was. The moment only, eternal.

Berkeley, 1980

AFTER PARADISE

Don't run anymore. Quiet. How softly it rains
On the roofs of the city. How perfect
All things are. Now, for the two of you
Waking up in a royal bed by a garret window.
For a man and a woman. For one plant divided
Into masculine and feminine which longed for each other.
Yes, this is my gift to you. Above ashes
On a bitter, bitter earth. Above the subterranean
Echo of clamorings and vows. So that now at dawn
You must be attentive: the tilt of a head,
A hand with a comb, two faces in a mirror
Are only forever once, even if unremembered,
So that you watch what is, though it fades away,
And are grateful every moment for your being.
Let that little park with greenish marble busts
In the pearl-gray light, under a summer drizzle,
Remain as it was when you opened the gate.
And the street of tall peeling porticoes
Which this love of yours suddenly transformed.

THE HOOKS OF A CORSET

In a big city, on the boulevards, early. The raising of jalousies and marquees, sprinkled slabs of sidewalk, echo of steps, the spotted bark of trees. My twentieth century was beginning and they walked, men and women; it is now close to its end and they walk, not exactly the same but pattering the same way with shoes and high-heeled slippers. The impenetrable order of a division into the male and female sex, into old and young, without decrease, always here, instead of those who once lived. And I, breathing the air, enchanted because I am one of them, identifying my flesh with their flesh, but at the same time aware of beings who might not have perished. I, replacing them, bearing a different name yet their own because the five senses are ours in common, I am walking here, now, before I am replaced in my turn. We are untouched by death and time, children, myself with Eve, in a kindergarten, in a sandbox, in a bed, embracing each other, making love, saying the words of eternal avowals and eternal delights. The space wide open, glittering machines up above, the rumble of the *métro* below. And our dresses under heaven, tinfoil crowns, tights, imitation animal hair, the scales of lizard-birds. To absorb with your eyes the inside of a flower shop, to hear the voices of people, to feel on your tongue the taste of just-drunk coffee. Passing by the windows of apartments, I invent stories, similar to my own, a lifted elbow, the combing of hair before a mirror. I multiplied myself and came to inhabit every one of them separately, thus my impermanence has no power over me.

❧

INSCRIPT

"And he sets off! and he watches the river of vitality flowing, so majestic and so brilliant. He admires the eternal beauty and astonishing harmony of life in the capitals, harmony so providentially maintained in the turmoil of human freedom. He contemplates the landscapes of big cities, landscapes caressed by mists or struck by the sun. He delights in beautiful carriages, proud horses, the spic-and-span cleanliness of grooms, the dexterity of footmen, the beauty of undulating women, in pretty children happy to be alive and well dressed; to put it briefly, in universal life. If a fashion, the cut of dresses changes slightly, if knotted ribbons or buckles are dethroned by a cockade, if the bonnet grows larger and the chignon descends to the nape of the neck, if the waistline goes up and the skirt is simplified, do not doubt that *his eagle's eye* even at a great distance will take notice. A regiment is passing, perhaps on its way to the end of the world, throwing into the air its enticing flourish, light as hope: and already Mr. G. saw, examined, analyzed the arms, the gait, and the physiognomy of that unit. Shoulder-belts, sparklings, music, resolute looks, heavy and ponderous moustaches, all that penetrates him pell-mell; and in a few minutes a poem which results from it will be composed. And already his soul lives with the life of that regiment which is marching as one animal, a proud image of joy in obedience!

"But evening comes. It is the bizarre and ambiguous hour when the curtains of the sky are drawn, when the cities light up. The gas makes a spot on the crimson of the sunset. Honest or dishonest, reasonable or crazy, people say to themselves: 'At last the day is over!' Wise men and rascals think of pleasure and everybody runs to a chosen place to drink the cup of oblivion. Mr. G. will remain to the last wherever the light still glows, poetry resounds, life teems, music vibrates; wherever a passion can pose for his eye, wherever the natural man and the man of convention show themselves in a strange beauty, wherever the sun witnesses the hurried pleasures of a *depraved animal.*"

—CHARLES BAUDELAIRE,
"Constantin Guys, Painter of Modern Life"

⚜

I am engaged in a serious operation, devoted to it exclusively, and for that reason I am released from the reproach of shirking my social duties. In the Quartier Latin, when bells ring for the New Year 1900, I am the one who walks uphill on rue Cujas. A gloved hand is linked to my arm and the gas hisses in the streetlamps. Her flesh which has turned to dust is as desirable to me as it was to that other man and if I touch her in my dream she does not even mention that she has died long ago. On the verge of a great discovery I almost penetrate the secret of the Particular transforming itself into the General and of the General transforming itself into the Particular. I endow with a philosophical meaning the moment when I helped her to undo the hooks of her corset.

⚘

INSCRIPT

"She was fond of tailored dresses from Vienna, very modest but rustling with linings made of iridescent taffeta; she would carry a rarely used lorgnon on a long chain interspersed with tiny pearls, and a bracelet with pendants. Her movements were slow and somewhat affected, she offered her hand to be kissed with a studied gesture, probably under her calm she was concealing the timidity characteristic of her whole family. Her jewelry, cigarette case, and perfume bore the stamp of an individual and fastidious taste. Her literary preferences were rather revolutionary and progressive. Much more vividly and sincerely than did Lela, she took an interest in her reading but in fact books were for her accessories to her dress, like a hat or an umbrella. Aunt Isia was the first to introduce Doroszewicze to the fashionable Tetmajer, then she brought the photographs of Ghirlandaio's and Botticelli's paintings from Italy and talked about the school of the early Renaissance, finally she took a liking to Przybyszewski and his style, and would often say: 'Do you want white peacocks?—I will give you white peacocks. Do you want crimson amethysts?—I will give you crimson amethysts.'"

—JANINA ŻÓŁTOWSKA,
Other Times, Other People (Inne czasy, inni ludzie)

Rustling taffetas. At sunset in a park by the Prypet River.
The party sets out for a walk on a path lined with flowers.
The fragrance of nicotianas, phlox, and resedas.
Great silence, the empty expanse of rising waters.
Meanwhile the servants bring in lamps, set the table for supper.
And the dining room windows lit the agaves on the lawn.

Lela, Marishka, Sophineta! Lenia, Stenia, Isia, Lilka!
Is it fair that I will never talk with you
In a language not disguised by etiquette
As less than language and not reduced to table chatter
But austere and precise like a thought
That attempts to embrace the poor lives of beings?

I walk about. No longer human. In a hunting outfit.
Visiting our thick forests and the houses and manors.
Cold borscht is served and I am abstracted
With disturbing questions from the end of my century,
Mainly regarding the truth, where does it come from, where is it?
Mum, I was eating chicken with cucumber salad.

My pretty ones, abducted, beyond will and guilt.
My awareness harrows me as well as my silence.
All my life I gathered up images and ideas,
I learned how to travel through lost territories,
But the moment between birth and disappearance
Is too much, I know, for the meager word.

Strings of wild ducks fly over the Respublica's waters.
Dew falls on Polish manners imported from Warsaw and Vienna.
I cross the river in a dugout to the village side.
Barking dogs greet me there and the bell of an Orthodox church.

What would I like to tell you? That I didn't get what I looked for:
To gather all of us naked on the earthly pastures
Under the endless light of suspended time
Without that form which confines me as it once confined you.

Seeing the future. A diviner. In a soft merciful night.
When pigweed grows on the paths of a cut-down garden
And a narrow gold chain on a white neck,
Together with the memory of all of you, perishes.

✧

INSCRIPT

"In the Ukraine several hundred gardens of various sizes survived the fall
of the Respublica and of the gentry whose presence was marked every-
where by old trees, lawns and decorative shrubbery. Once, in the eastern
Carpathians, in a remote valley distant by a whole day's walk from the
nearest settlement, I noticed, lost among hazels, one of those decorative
shrubs characteristic of gardens from the beginning of the last century.
Parting raspberries and vines I found a few old stones and bricks. Even
in that wilderness the settlers had remained faithful to the horticultural
passion of the old Respublica."

—PAWEŁ HOSTOWIEC,
In the Valley of the Dniester (W dolinie Dniestru)

What did I really want to tell them? That I labored to transcend my place
and time, searching for the Real. And here is my work done (commend-
ably?), my life fulfilled, as it was destined to be, in grief. Now I appear to
myself as one who was under the delusion of being his own while he was
the subject of a style. Just as they were, so what if it was a different subjec-
tion. "Do you want white peacocks?—I will give you white peacocks."

And we could have been united only by what we have in common: the same nakedness in a garden beyond time, but the moments are short when it seems to me that, at odds with time, we hold each other's hands. And I drink wine and I shake my head and say: "What man feels and thinks will never be expressed."

ANNALENA

It happened that sometimes I kissed in mirrors the reflection of my face; since the hands, face and tears of Annalena had caressed it, my face seemed to me divinely beautiful and as if suffused with heavenly sweetness.

—O. Milosz, *L'Amoureuse Initiation*

I liked your velvet yoni, Annalena, long voyages in the delta of your legs.

A striving upstream toward your beating heart through more and more savage currents saturated with the light of hops and bindweed.

And our vehemence and triumphant laughter and our hasty dressing in the middle of the night to walk on the stone stairs of the upper city.

Our breath held by amazement and silence, porosity of worn-out stones and the great door of the cathedral.

Over the gate of the rectory fragments of brick among weeds, in darkness the touch of a rough buttressed wall.

And later our looking from the bridge down to the orchard, when under the moon every tree is separate on its kneeler, and from the secret interior of dimmed poplars the echo carries the sound of a water turbine.

To whom do we tell what happened on the earth, for whom do we place everywhere huge mirrors in the hope that they will be filled up and will stay so?

Always in doubt whether it was we who were there, you and I, Annalena, or just anonymous lovers on the enameled tablets of a fairyland.

YELLOW BICYCLE

When I ask her what she wants,
She says, "A yellow bicycle."
                                    —Robert Hass

As long as we move at a dancing gait, my love,
Leaving the car by the place where a yellow bicycle stands, leaning
    against a tree,
As long as we enter the gardens at a dancing gait,
Northern gardens, full of dew and the voices of birds,
Our memory is childish and it saves only what we need:
Yesterday morning and evening, no further.
But then we recalled a girl who had a yellow bicycle like that
And used to talk to it in caressing words.
Later on, among flower beds between box hedges,
We saw a little statue and a plate with the sculptor's name.
We were descending by terraces toward a lake
Which is like a lake from an old ballad,
Smooth, between the peninsulas of spruce forests.
Thus common human memory visited us again.

WINTER

The pungent smells of a California winter,
Grayness and rosiness, an almost transparent full moon.
I add logs to the fire, I drink and I ponder.

"In Ilawa," the news item said, "at age 70
Died Aleksander Rymkiewicz, poet."

He was the youngest in our group. I patronized him slightly,
Just as I patronized others for their inferior minds
Though they had many virtues I couldn't touch.

And so I am here, approaching the end
Of the century and of my life. Proud of my strength
Yet embarrassed by the clearness of the view.

Avant-gardes mixed with blood.
The ashes of inconceivable arts.
An omnium-gatherum of chaos.

I passed judgment on that. Though marked myself.
This hasn't been the age for the righteous and the decent.
I know what it means to beget monsters
And to recognize in them myself.

You, moon, You, Aleksander, fire of cedar logs.
Waters close over us, a name lasts but an instant.
Not important whether the generations hold us in memory.
Great was that chase with the hounds for the unattainable meaning of
    the world.

And now I am ready to keep running
When the sun rises beyond the borderlands of death.

I already see mountain ridges in the heavenly forest
Where, beyond every essence, a new essence waits.

You, music of my late years, I am called
By a sound and a color which are more and more perfect.

Do not die out, fire. Enter my dreams, love.
Be young forever, seasons of the earth.

AT DAWN

How enduring, how we need durability.
The sky before sunrise is soaked with light.
Rosy color tints buildings, bridges, and the Seine.
I was here when she, with whom I walk, wasn't born yet
And the cities on a distant plain stood intact
Before they rose in the air with the dust of sepulchral brick
And the people who lived there didn't know.
Only this moment at dawn is real to me.
The bygone lives are like my own past life, uncertain.
I cast a spell on the city asking it to last.

THE CITY

The city exulted, all in flowers.
Soon it will end: a fashion, a phase, the epoch, life.
The terror and sweetness of a final dissolution.
Let the first bombs fall without delay.

ANKA

In what hat, from what epoch,
Is Anka posing in the photograph,
Above her brow the wing of a killed bird?
Now she is one of them, beyond the threshold
Where there are no men, no women,
And the prophet does not give separate sermons
To the ones covered with shawls
So that their long hair does not provoke lust,
And to the tanned, bearded men in draped burnouses.
Saved from the furnaces of World War II,
Trying on dresses in reflected mirrors
And blouses and necklaces and rings,
With a hairstyle and makeup for the wars of her career,
Happy to go to bed or just talk over wine,
The owner of a beautiful apartment, full of sculpture.
Left to herself till the end of the world,
How does she manage now, fleshless?
And what could the prophet find to say, when he has no thought
Of the hair under a shawl and the secret
Fragrance of skin and of ointments?

THEODICY

No, it won't do, my sweet theologians.
Desire will not save the morality of God.
If he created beings able to choose between good and evil,
And they chose, and the world lies in iniquity,
Nevertheless, there is pain, and the undeserved torture of creatures,
Which would find its explanation only by assuming
The existence of an archetypal Paradise
And a pre-human downfall so grave
That the world of matter received its shape from diabolic power.

TABLE I

Only this table is certain. Heavy. Of massive wood.
At which we are feasting as others have before us,
Sensing under the varnish the touch of other fingers.
Everything else is doubtful. We too, appearing
For a moment in the guise of men or women
(Why either-or?), in preordained dress.
I stare at her, as if for the first time.
And at him. And at her. So that I can recall them
In what unearthly latitude or kingdom?
Preparing myself for what moment?
For what departure from among the ashes?
If I am here, entire, if I am cutting meat
In this tavern by the wobbly splendor of the sea.

TABLE II

In a tavern by the wobbly splendor of the sea,
I move as in an aquarium, aware of disappearing,
For we are all so mortal that we hardly live.
I am pleased by this union, even if funereal,
Of sights, gestures, touches, now and in ages past.
I believed my entreaties would bring time to a standstill.
I learned compliance, as others did before me.
And I only examine what endures here:
The knives with horn handles, the tin basins,
Blue porcelain, strong though brittle,
And, like a rock embattled in the flow
And polished to a gloss, this table of heavy wood.

MY-NESS

"My parents, my husband, my brother, my sister."
I am listening in a cafeteria at breakfast.
The women's voices rustle, fulfill themselves
In a ritual no doubt necessary.
I glance sidelong at their moving lips
And I delight in being here on earth
For one more moment, with them, here on earth,
To celebrate our tiny, tiny my-ness.

To find my home in one sentence, concise, as if hammered in metal. Not to enchant anybody. Not to earn a lasting name in posterity. An unnamed need for order, for rhythm, for form, which three words are opposed to chaos and nothingness.

Berkeley–Paris–Cambridge, Massachusetts, 1981–1983

IN A JAR

Now, with all my knowledge, honorable newts,
I approach the jar in which you live
And see how you float up vertically to the surface
Showing your bellies of vermilion color,
Color of flame, that makes you akin
To the alchemists' salamander living in fire.
Perhaps that's the reason why I caught you
In a pond between pines when white April clouds race,
And carried you to town, proud of my trophy.
You vanished so long ago, I ponder the moment
When you lived unaware of hours and years.
I address you, I give you existence—
Even a name and a title in the princedom of grammar—
To protect you by inflection from nothingness.
Myself no doubt held by powers who observe me
And transfer me to some grammatical hyper-form,
While I wait with the hope that they seize me and carry me up
So that I last like an alchemists' salamander in fire.

South Hadley, 1985

MARY MAGDALEN AND I

The seven unclean spirits of Mary Magdalen
Chased from her by the Teacher with his prayer
Hover in the air in a bat-like flight,
While she, with one leg folded in,
Another bent at the knee, sits staring hard
At her toe and the thong of her sandal
As if she had just noticed such an odd thing.
Her chestnut-brown hair curls in rings
And covers her back, strong, almost virile,
Resting on her shoulder, on a dark-blue dress
Under which her nakedness phosphoresces.
The face is heavyish, the neck harboring
A voice that is low, husky, as if hoarse.
But she will say nothing. Forever between
The element of flesh and the element
Of hope, she stays still. At the canvas's corner
The name of a painter who desired her.

Berkeley, 1985

A CONFESSION

My Lord, I loved strawberry jam
And the dark sweetness of a woman's body.
Also well-chilled vodka, herring in olive oil,
Scents, of cinnamon, of cloves.
So what kind of prophet am I? Why should the spirit
Have visited such a man? Many others
Were justly called, and trustworthy.
Who would have trusted me? For they saw
How I empty glasses, throw myself on food,
And glance greedily at the waitress's neck.
Flawed and aware of it. Desiring greatness,
Able to recognize greatness wherever it is,
And yet not quite, only in part, clairvoyant,
I knew what was left for smaller men like me:
A feast of brief hopes, a rally of the proud,
A tournament of hunchbacks, literature.

Berkeley, 1985

WITH HER

Those poor, arthritically swollen knees
Of my mother in an absent country.
I think of them on my seventy-fourth birthday
As I attend early Mass at St. Mary Magdalen in Berkeley.
A reading this Sunday from the Book of Wisdom
About how God has not made death
And does not rejoice in the annihilation of the living.
A reading from the Gospel according to Mark
About a little girl to whom He said: "Talitha, cumi!"
This is for me. To make me rise from the dead
And repeat the hope of those who lived before me,
In a fearful unity with her, with her pain of dying,
In a village near Danzig, in a dark November,
When both the mournful Germans, old men and women,
And the evacuees from Lithuania would fall ill with typhus.
Be with me, I say to her, my time has been short.
Your words are now mine, deep inside me:
"It all seems now to have been a dream."

Berkeley, 1985

1945

—You! the last Polish poet!—drunk, he embraced me,
My friend from the Avant-Garde, in a long military coat,
Who had lived through the war in Russia and, there, understood.

He could not have learned those things from Apollinaire,
Or Cubist manifestos, or the festivals of Paris streets.
The best cure for illusions is hunger, patience, and obedience.

In their fine capitals they still liked to talk.
Yet the twentieth century went on. It was not they
Who would decide what words were going to mean.

On the steppe, as he was binding his bleeding feet with a rag
He grasped the futile pride of those lofty generations.
As far as he could see, a flat, unredeemed earth.

Gray silence settled over every tribe and people.
After the bells of baroque churches, after a hand on a saber,
After disputes over free will, and arguments of diets.

I blinked, ridiculous and rebellious,
Alone with my Jesus Mary against irrefutable power,
A descendant of ardent prayers, of gilded sculptures and miracles.

And I knew I would speak in the language of the vanquished
No more durable than old customs, family rituals,
Christmas tinsel, and once a year the hilarity of carols.

Berkeley, 1985

FEAR-DREAM (1918)

Orsha is a bad station. In Orsha a train risks stopping for days.
Thus perhaps in Orsha I, six years old, got lost
And the repatriation train was starting, about to leave me behind,
Forever. As if I grasped that I would have been somebody else,
A poet of another language, of a different fate.
As if I guessed my end at the shores of Kolyma
Where the bottom of the sea is white with human skulls.
And a great dread visited me then,
The one destined to be the mother of all my fears.

A trembling of the small before the great. Before the Empire.
Which constantly marches westward, armed with bows, lariats, rifles,
Riding in a troika, pummeling the driver's back,
Or in a jeep, wearing fur hats, with a file full of conquered countries.
And I just flee, for a hundred, three hundred years,
On the ice, swimming across, by day, by night, on and on.
Abandoning by my river a punctured cuirass and a coffer with king's
    grants.
Beyond the Dnieper, then the Niemen, then the Bug and the Vistula.

Finally I arrive in a city of high houses and long streets
And am oppressed by fear, for I am just a villager
Who only pretends to follow what they discuss so shrewdly
And tries to hide from them his shame, his defeat.

Who will feed me here, as I walk in the cloudy dawn
With small change in my pocket, for one coffee, no more?
A refugee from fictitious States, who will want me here?

Stony walls, indifferent walls, bitter walls.
By order of their reason, not my reason.
Now accept it. Don't kick. You are not going to flee any further.

Berkeley, 1985

SIX LECTURES IN VERSE

Lecture I

How to tell it all? Referring to what chronicles?
Imagine a young man walking by a lake shore
On a hot afternoon. Dragonflies, diaphanous,
Over the rushes as always. But nothing of what's to come
Has yet arrived. Understand: nothing.
Or perhaps it has, but is unfulfilled.
Bodies assigned for wounds, cities for destruction,
Pain of uncounted numbers, each pain one's own.
Concrete for crematoria, States for partitioning,
Assassins drawn by lot: you, and you, and you.
Yes. And the jet. The transistor. The video.
Men on the moon. He walks and doesn't know.

He comes to a little bay, a kind of beach.
People on vacation are there sunbathing.
Gentlemen and ladies, bored, talk about
Who is sleeping with whom, bridge, and a new tango.
That young man is me. I was him, perhaps still am
Though half a century has passed. I remember and don't remember
How they and he were at odds. He is different, alien.
Prisoners of his mind, they flash by and vanish.
He scorns them, a judge, observer.
Thus the sickliness of adolescence
Divines the sickness of an era
That will not end well. Those who are unaware
Deserve to be punished: they wanted only to live.

A wave, bits of reed on gravel, white clouds.
Beyond the water, village roofs, a wood. And imagination.
In it, Jewish towns, a train crossing the flatlands.
Abyss. The earth is swaying. Does it sway only now
When I throw open the labyrinths of time,

As if to know meant to comprehend,
And beyond the window hummingbirds perform their dance?

I should have . . . I should have what fifty-five years ago?
I should have lived in joy. In harmony. In faith. In peace.
As if that had been possible. And later, stupefaction:
Why hadn't they been wiser? It all appears now as a sequence
Of cause and effect. No, that too is doubtful.
Everyone's responsible who ever breathed—
Air? Unreason? Illusion? Idea?
Like everyone who lived there and then, I didn't see clearly.
This I confess to you, my young students.

Lecture II

Mothers and sisters, tender wives and lovers.
Think of them. They lived and had names.
I saw on a radiant Adriatic beach
Between the Wars, a girl so beautiful
I wanted to stop her in the irrevocable moment.
Her slenderness clasped by a silk bathing suit
(Before the era of plastic), color of indigo
Or ultramarine. Her eyes, violet,
Hair, blond touched with russet. Daughter of patricians,
Of a lordly clan perhaps, striding confidently.
Fair-haired young men, as handsome as she,
Served as her retinue. Sigrid or Inge
From a house scented with cigars, well-being, order.

"Don't go off, fool. Better to take refuge
In hieratic sculptures, church mosaics, rosy gold auroras.
Stay as an echo on waters at sunset.
Don't destroy yourself, don't trust. Not splendor and glory,
But an apish circus calls you, your tribal rite."

So I could have told her. An essence, a person?
A soul, unique? While day of birth
And place of birth, like a planetary house,
Control what she'll be: seduced by her love
Of native customs, by her obedient virtue.

Dante was wrong, alas. It doesn't happen that way.
The verdict is collective. Eternal damnation
Should have afflicted all of them, yes, all.
Which is no doubt impossible. Jesus has to face
Flowery teapots, coffee, philosophizing,
Landscapes with deer, the sound of the clock on the town hall.
Nobody will be convinced by him, black-eyed,
A hooked nose, the dirty clothes
Of a convict or slave, one of those drifters
The State justly catches and disposes of.
Now, when I know so much, I have to forgive
My own transgressions, not unlike theirs:
I wanted to equal others, behave just like them.
To shut my ears, not to hear the call of prophets.
That's why I understand her. A snug home, a garden,
And from the depths of Hell, a fugue of Bach.

Lecture III

Poor humanity is camping on train station floors.
Caps with earflaps, babushkas, quilted jackets, sheepskins.
They sleep side by side, waiting for a train. Cold blows in through the
    doorway.
New arrivals shake off snow, adding to the mud.

I know it's not for you, that knowledge of Smolensk, Saratov.
And better it is not. If one can, let him avoid

Compassion, that ache of imagination.
So I won't labor this. Just fragments, an outline.
They appear. The guards. Three men and one woman.
The leather of their long boots is soft, first-class,
Coats of expensive fur. Movements arrogant, confident.
Leading on leash their German shepherds. Look at her,
Large, still sleepy, well fucked in bed,
Glancing scornfully from under a beaver cap.
Doesn't she clearly show who holds the power here,
Who takes the prize? Ideological,
If you prefer. For nothing here is professed,
All is disguised in a ritual phrase,
Though the fear is real, people obedient,
And where are these four coming from, in a snowstorm,
Real barbed wire, watchtowers of a camp.

At the Congress for the Defense of Culture in Paris
In spring 1935, my fellow student,
Wandering across Europe, Günther from Marburg,
Chuckled. An admirer of Stefan George,
He would write poems on knightly valor
And carried a pocket edition of Nietzsche.
He was to die, perhaps near Smolensk.
From whose bullet? One of those here asleep.
The guard with the dogs? A camp inmate?
This Nadia or Irina? About them, he knew nothing.

Lecture IV

Reality, what can we do with it? Where is it in words?
Just as it flickers, it vanishes. Innumerable lives
Unremembered. Cities on maps only,
Without that face in the window, on the first floor, by the market,

Without those two in the bushes near the gas plant.
Returning seasons, mountain snows, oceans,
And the blue ball of the Earth rotates,
But silent are they who ran through artillery fire,
Who clung to a lump of clay for protection,
And those deported from their homes at dawn
And those who have crawled out from under a pile of bodies,
While here, I, an instructor in forgetting,
Teach that pain passes (for it's the pain of others),
Still in my mind trying to save Miss Jadwiga,
A little hunchback, librarian by profession,
Who perished in the shelter of an apartment house
That was considered safe but toppled down
And no one was able to dig through the slabs of wall,
Though knocking and voices were heard for many days.
So a name is lost for ages, forever,
No one will ever know about her last hours,
Time carries her in layers of the Pliocene.
The true enemy of man is generalization.
The true enemy of man, so-called History,
Attracts and terrifies with its plural number.
Don't believe it. Cunning and treacherous,
History is not, as Marx told us, anti-nature,
And if a goddess, a goddess of blind fate.
The little skeleton of Miss Jadwiga, the spot
Where her heart was pulsating. This only
I set against necessity, law, theory.

Lecture V

"Christ has risen." Whoever believes that
Should not behave as we do,
Who have lost the up, the down, the right, the left, heavens, abysses,

And try somehow to muddle on, in cars, in beds,
Men clutching at women, women clutching at men,
Falling, rising, putting coffee on the table,
Buttering bread, for here's another day.

And another year. Time to exchange presents.
Christmas trees aglow, music,
All of us, Presbyterians, Lutherans, Catholics,
Like to sit in the pew, sing with others,
Give thanks for being here together still,
For the gift of echoing the Word, now and in all ages.

We rejoice at having been spared the misfortune
Of countries where, as we read, the enslaved
Kneel before the idol of the State, live and die with its name
On their lips, not knowing they're enslaved.
However that may be, The Book is always with us,
And in it, miraculous signs, counsels, orders.
Unhygienic, it's true, and contrary to common sense,
But they exist and that's enough on the mute earth.
It's as if a fire warmed us in a cave
While outside the golden rain of stars is motionless.
Theologians are silent. And philosophers
Don't even dare ask: "What is truth?"
And so, after the great wars, undecided,
With almost good will but not quite,
We plod on with hope. And now let everyone
Confess to himself. "Has he risen?" "I don't know."

Lecture VI

Boundless history lasted in that moment
When he was breaking bread and drinking wine.

They were being born, they desired, they died.
My God, what crowds! How is it possible
That all of them wanted to live and are no more?

A teacher leads a flock of five-year-olds
Through the marble halls of a museum.
She seats them on the floor, polite boys
And girls, facing a huge painting,
And explains: "A helmet, a sword, the gods,
A mountain, white clouds, an eagle, lightning."
She is knowing, they see for the first time.
Her fragile throat, her female organs,
Her multicolored dress, creams, and trinkets
Are embraced by forgiveness. What is not embraced
By forgiveness? Lack of knowledge, innocent unconcern
Would cry for vengeance, demand a verdict
Had I been a judge. I won't be, I'm not.
In splendor the earth's poor moment renews itself.
Simultaneously, now, here, every day
Bread is changed into flesh, wine into blood,
And the impossible, what no one can bear,
Is again accepted and acknowledged.

I'm consoling you, of course. Consoling myself also.
Not very much consoled. Trees-candelabra
Carry their green candles. And magnolias bloom.

This too is real. The din ceases.
Memory closes down its dark waters.
And those, as if behind a glass, stare out, silent.

Berkeley, 1985

AND YET THE BOOKS

And yet the books will be there on the shelves, separate beings,
That appeared once, still wet
As shining chestnuts under a tree in autumn,
And, touched, coddled, began to live
In spite of fires on the horizon, castles blown up,
Tribes on the march, planets in motion.
"We are," they said, even as their pages
Were being torn out, or a buzzing flame
Licked away their letters. So much more durable
Than we are, whose frail warmth
Cools down with memory, disperses, perishes.
I imagine the earth when I am no more:
Nothing happens, no loss, it's still a strange pageant,
Women's dresses, dewy lilacs, a song in the valley.
Yet the books will be there on the shelves, well born,
Derived from people, but also from radiance, heights.

Berkeley, 1986

ON PARTING WITH MY WIFE, JANINA

Women mourners were giving their sister to fire.
And fire, the same as we looked at together,
She and I, in marriage through long years,
Bound by an oath for good or ill, fire
In fireplaces in winter, campfires, fires of burning cities,
Elemental, pure, from the beginnings of the Earth,
Was taking away her streaming hair, gray,
Seized her lips and her neck, engulfed her, fire
That in human languages designates love.
I thought nothing of languages. Or of words of prayer.

I loved her, without knowing who she really was.
I inflicted pain on her, chasing my illusion.
I betrayed her with women, though faithful to her only.
We lived through much happiness and unhappiness,
Separations, miraculous rescues. And now, this ash.
And the sea battering the shore when I walk the empty boulevard.
And the sea battering the shore. And ordinary sorrow.

How to resist nothingness? What power
Preserves what once was, if memory does not last?
For I remember little. I remember so very little.
Indeed, moments restored would mean the Last Judgment
That is adjourned from day to day, by Mercy perhaps.

Fire, liberation from gravity. An apple does not fall,
A mountain moves from its place. Beyond the fire-curtain,
A lamb stands in the meadow of indestructible forms.
The souls in Purgatory burn. Heraclitus, crazy,
Sees the flame consuming the foundations of the world.
Do I believe in the Resurrection of the Flesh? Not of this ash.

I call, I beseech: elements, dissolve yourselves!
Rise into the other, let it come, kingdom!
Beyond the earthly fire compose yourselves anew!

Berkeley, 1986

BLACKSMITH SHOP

I liked the bellows operated by rope.
A hand or foot pedal—I don't remember which.
But that blowing, and the blazing of the fire!
And a piece of iron in the fire, held there by tongs,
Red, softened for the anvil,
Beaten with a hammer, bent into a horseshoe,
Thrown in a bucket of water, sizzle, steam.

And horses hitched to be shod,
Tossing their manes; and in the grass by the river
Plowshares, sledge runners, harrows waiting for repair

At the entrance, my bare feet on the dirt floor,
Here, gusts of heat; at my back, white clouds.
I stare and stare. It seems I was called for this:
To glorify things just because they are.

ADAM AND EVE

Adam and Eve were reading about a monkey in a bath,
Who jumped into the tub, imitating her mistress
And started to turn faucets: Aï, boiling hot!
The lady arrives running, in a robe, her white breasts,
Huge, with a blue vein, dangle.
She rescues the monkey, sits at her dressing table,
Calls for her maid, it's time to go to church.

And not only about that were Adam and Eve reading,
Resting a book on their naked knees.
Those castles! Those palaces! Those towering cities!
Planetary airfields between pagodas!
They looked at each other, smiled,
Though uncertainly (you will be, you will know)
And the hand of Eve reached for the apple.

LINNAEUS

He was born in 1707 at 1:00 a.m. on May 23rd,
when spring was in beautiful bloom, and cuckoo
had just announced the coming of summer.

—From Linnaeus's biography

Green young leaves. A cuckoo. Echo.
To get up at four in the morning, to run to the river
Which steams, smooth under the rising sun.
A gate is open, horses are running,
Swallows dart, fish splash. And did we not begin with an overabundance
Of glitterings and calls, pursuits and trills?
We lived every day in hymn, in rapture,
Not finding words, just feeling it is too much.

He was one of us, happy in our childhood.
He would set out with his botanic box
To gather and to name, like Adam in the garden
Who did not finish his task, expelled too early.
Nature has been waiting for names ever since:
On the meadows near Uppsala, white, at dusk
Platanthera is fragrant, he called it *bifolia*.
Turdus sings in a spruce thicket, but is it *musicus*?
That must remain the subject of dispute.
And the botanist laughed at a little perky bird
For ever *Troglodytes troglodytes L.*

He arranged three kingdoms into a system.
Animale. Vegetale. Minerale.
He divided: classes, orders, genuses, species.
"How manifold are Thy works, O Jehovah!"
He would sing with the psalmist. Rank, number, symmetry
Are everywhere, praised with a clavecin
And violin, scanned in Latin hexameter.

Ever since we have had the language of marvel: atlases.
A tulip with its dark, mysterious inside,
Anemones of Lapland, a water lily, an iris
Faithfully portrayed by a scrupulous brush.
And a bird in foliage, russet and dark blue,
Never flies off, retained
On the page with an ornate double inscription.

We were grateful to him. In the evenings at home
We contemplated colors under a kerosene lamp
With a green shade. And what there, on earth,
Was unattainable, over much, passing away, perishing,
Here we could love, safe from loss.

May his household, orangery, the garden
In which he grew plants from overseas
Be blessed with peace and well-being.
To China and Japan, America, Australia,
Sailing-ships carried his disciples;
They would bring back gifts: seeds and drawings.
And I, who in this bitter age deprived of harmony
Am a wanderer and a gatherer of visible forms,
Envying them, bring to him my tribute—
A verse imitating the classical ode.

MISTER HANUSEVICH

Hanusevich wants Nina. But why? Why?
He has tantrums, blubbers when drunk.
Nina laughs. Is he not funny?
Fat and all nerves, he has big ears
And flaps them, a real elephant.

A dark-blue cloud stands over San Francisco
When I drive along Grizzly Peak,
And far out, beyond the Golden Gate, the ocean gleamed.

Aï, my dead of long ago! Aï, Hanusevich, aï, Nina!
Nobody remembers you, nobody knows about you.

Hanusevich had his estate somewhere near Minsk.
The region was taken by the Bolsheviks, so he lives in Wilno.
When he was young, his mommy let him have flings.
He caroused with chanteuses, pretended to be a big shot,
Would send telegrams in Russian: *"Arriving with ladies*
Meet with music troikas champagne"
And a signature: *Count Bobrinskii.*

Chanteuses. I see now their satin underskirts
And black panties with lace. Breasts, too big, too small,
Worries, touching themselves in mirrors, tardy menses.
Later on they changed into *sestritsas* in the windows of hospital trains
(On their brows, bound with a veil, the sign of the red cross).

Nina is not for Hanusevich. Look how she walks.
She rolls from side to side, like a sailor.
A whole year in the saddle, in a cavalry regiment.
What sort of marriageable young lady is she?

What did you find in her, Mister Hanusevich
That you got so romantic? Always pretending,

Perhaps you adorned her with your fantasies.
And, it is true, your funny ears
Nearly transparent, with red veins,
Move, and in your eyes, nearly always, fright.

Once upon a time there was Hanusevich. And there was Nina.
Once only, from the beginning till the end of the world.
It is I who perform, late, this ceremonial wedding.
And around me striped, emerald-eyed beasts,
Ladies from journals of fashion, shamans of lost tribes,
Or, with a secret smile, a grave *sestritsa,*
Appear among white clouds, assist.

THE THISTLE, THE NETTLE

Let the sad terrestrials remember me,
recognize me and salute: the thistle and the tall nettle,
and the childhood enemy, belladonna.

—O. V. de L. Milosz, "Les Terrains Vagues"

The thistle, the nettle, the burdock, and belladonna
Have a future. Theirs are wastelands
And rusty railroad tracks, the sky, silence.

Who shall I be for men many generations later?
When, after the clamor of tongues, the award goes to silence?

I was to be redeemed by the gift of arranging words
But must be prepared for an earth without grammar,

For the thistle, the nettle, the burdock, the belladonna,
And a small wind above them, a sleepy cloud, silence.

IN COMMON

What is good? Garlic. A leg of lamb on a spit.
Wine with a view of boats rocking in a cove.
A starry sky in August. A rest on a mountain peak.

What is good? After a long drive water in a pool and a sauna.
Lovemaking and falling asleep, embraced, your legs touching hers.
Mist in the morning, translucent, announcing a sunny day.

I am submerged in everything that is common to us, the living.
Experiencing this earth for them, in my flesh.
Walking past the vague outline of skyscrapers? anti-temples?
In valleys of beautiful, though poisoned, rivers.

CONVERSATION WITH JEANNE

Let us not talk philosophy, drop it, Jeanne.
So many words, so much paper, who can stand it.
I told you the truth about my distancing myself.
I've stopped worrying about my misshapen life.
It was no better and no worse than the usual human tragedies.

For over thirty years we have been waging our dispute
As we do now, on the island under the skies of the tropics.
We flee a downpour, in an instant the bright sun again,
And I grow dumb, dazzled by the emerald essence of the leaves.

We submerge in foam at the line of the surf,
We swim far, to where the horizon is a tangle of banana bush,
With little windmills of palms.
And I am under accusation: That I am not up to my oeuvre,
That I do not demand enough from myself,
As I could have learned from Karl Jaspers,
That my scorn for the opinions of this age grows slack.

I roll on a wave and look at white clouds.

You are right, Jeanne, I don't know how to care about the salvation of
    my soul.
Some are called, others manage as well as they can.
I accept it, what has befallen me is just.
I don't pretend to the dignity of a wise old age.
Untranslatable into words, I chose my home in what is now,
In things of this world, which exist and, for that reason, delight us:
Nakedness of women on the beach, coppery cones of their breasts,
Hibiscus, alamanda, a red lily, devouring
With my eyes, lips, tongue.
Guava juice, the juice of *la prune de Cythère,*
Rum with ice and syrup, lianas–orchids
In a rain forest, where trees stand on the stilts of their roots.

Death you say, mine and yours, closer and closer,
We suffered and this poor earth was not enough.
The purple-black earth of vegetable gardens
Will be here, either looked at or not.
The sea, as today, will breathe from its depths.
Growing small, I disappear in the immense, more and more free.

Guadeloupe, 1991

ON A BEACH

The sea breaks on the sands, I listen to its surge and close my eyes,

Here on this European shore, in the fullness of summer, after the big wars of the century.

The brows of new generations are innocent, yet marked.

Often in a crowd a face resembling—he could be one of the destroyers

If he were born a little earlier but he doesn't know it.

Chosen, as his father was, though not called.

Under my eyelids I keep their eternally young cities.

The shouts of their music, the rock pulsating, I am searching for the core of my thought.

Is it only what can't be expressed, the "ah" mumbled every day—:

The irretrievable, indifferent, eternal vanishing?

Is it pity and anger because after the ecstasy and despair and hope beings similar to gods are swallowed by oblivion?

Because in the sea's surging and silences one hears nothing about a division into the just and the wicked?

Or was I pursued by images of those who were alive for a day, an hour, a moment, under the skies?

So much, and now the peace of defeat, for my verse has preserved so little?

Or perhaps I have only heard myself whispering: "Epilogue, epilogue"?

Prophecies of my youth fulfilled but not in the way one expected.

The morning is back, and flowers are gathered in the cool of the garden by a loving hand.

A flock of pigeons soars above the valley. They turn and change color flying along the mountains.

Same glory of ordinary days and milk in a jug and crisp cherries.

And yet down below, in the very brushwood of existence, it lurks and crawls,

Recognizable by the fluttering dread of small creatures, it, implacable, steel-gray nothingness.

⚘

I open my eyes, a ball flies past, a red sail leans on a wave which is blue in the gaudy sun.

Just before me a boy tests the water with his foot, and suddenly I notice he is not like others.

Not crippled, yet he has the movements of a cripple and the head of a retarded child.

His father looks after him, that handsome man sitting there on a boulder.

A sensation of my neighbor's misfortune pierces me and I begin to comprehend

In this dark age the bond of our common fate and a compassion more real than I was inclined to confess.

DECEMBER 1

The vineyard country, russet, reddish, carmine-brown in this season.
A blue outline of hills above a fertile valley.
It's warm as long as the sun does not set, in the shade cold returns.
A strong sauna and then swimming in a pool surrounded by trees.
Dark redwoods, transparent pale-leaved birches.
In their delicate network, a sliver of the moon.
I describe this for I have learned to doubt philosophy
And the visible world is all that remains.

MEANING

—When I die, I will see the lining of the world.
The other side, beyond bird, mountain, sunset.
The true meaning, ready to be decoded.
What never added up will add up,
What was incomprehensible will be comprehended.

—And if there is no lining to the world?
If a thrush on a branch is not a sign,
But just a thrush on the branch? If night and day
Make no sense following each other?
And on this earth there is nothing except this earth?

—Even if that is so, there will remain
A word wakened by lips that perish,
A tireless messenger who runs and runs
Through interstellar fields, through the revolving galaxies,
And calls out, protests, screams.

KAZIA

A two-horse wagon was covered with tarpaulin stretched on boughs of hazel and in that manner we had been voyaging a couple of days, while my eyes kept starting out of my head from curiosity. Especially when we left the flat region of fields and woods for a country of hills and many lakes, which I was to learn later was shaped thus by a glacier. That country revealed to me something not named, what might be called today a peaceful husbandry of man on the earth: the smoke of villages, cattle coming back from pasture, mowers with their scythes cutting oats and after-grasses, here and there a rowboat near the shore, rocked gently by a wave. Undoubtedly these things existed also elsewhere, but here they were somehow condensed into one modest space of everyday rituals and labors.

We were hospitably received for the night in a manor by a lake. My memory stops at the very border of returning there but cannot cross it and the name of the place does not appear, nor the name of our hosts, nothing except the name, Kazia, of that little girl at whom I looked, about whom I thought something, though how she looked I do not know anymore, all I know is that she was wearing a sailor's collar.

And so it is, against expectation, that Kazia or another girl, a complete stranger, accompanies us for years and we constantly ask ourselves what happened to her. For, after all, we are able, by concentrating our attention, to raise her, so to say, to the square and to make her important to us disinterestedly, since nothing sentimental colors our imaginings. This is a meditation on one of our contemporaries, how she did not choose a place or time to be born into such and such family. There is no help, I entangle her in everything that has happened since that moment, thus, the history of the century, of the country, of that region. Let us assume that she married, had a child, then was deported to Asia, starving, infected with lice, tried to save herself and her child, worked hard, discovering a dimension of existence which is better left in silence, for our notions of decency and morality have nothing to do with it. Let us assume she learned about the death of her husband in a gulag, found herself in

Iran, had two husbands more, lived successively in Africa, in England, in America. And the house by the lake followed her in her dreams. Of course in my fantasies I imagine a day and a place of our meeting as two adults, which has never occurred, perhaps our affair, her nakedness, her hair, dark I am pretty certain, our basic resemblance, of a couple having the same tribe, language, manners. We have been paying too much attention to what separates people; in truth we could have been, we, the two of us, married, and it would have been fine, and our biographies would have faded in human memory as they fade now, when I have no idea what she really felt and thought, and am unable to describe it.

CAPRI

I am a child who receives First Communion in Wilno and afterwards drinks cocoa served by zealous Catholic ladies.

I am an old man who remembers that day in June: the ecstasy of the sinless, white tablecloth and the sun on vases filled with peonies.

Qu'as tu fait, qu'as tu fait de ta vie?—voices call, in various languages gathered in your wanderings through two continents. What did you do with your life, what did you do?

Slowly, cautiously, now when destiny is fulfilled I enter the scenes of the bygone time,

Of my century, in which, and not in any other, I was ordered to be born, to work, and to leave a trace.

Those Catholic ladies existed, after all, and if I returned there now, identical but with another consciousness, I would look intensely at their faces, trying to prevent their fading away.

Also, carriages and rumps of horses illuminated by lightning or by the pulsating flow of distant artillery.

Chimneyless huts, smoke billowing on their roofs, and wide sandy roads in pine forests.

Countries and cities that must remain without name, for how can I explain why and how many times they changed their banners and emblems?

Early we receive a call, yet it remains incomprehensible, and only late do we discover how obedient we were.

The river rolls its waters past, as it did long ago, the church of St. Jacob, I am there together with my foolishness, which is shameful, but had I been wiser it would not have helped.

Now I know foolishness is necessary in all our designs, so that they are realized, awkwardly and incompletely.

And this river, together with heaps of garbage on its banks, with the beginning of pollution, flows through my youth, a warning against the longing for ideal places on the earth.

Yet, there, on that river, I experienced full happiness, a ravishment beyond any thought or concern, still lasting in my body.

Just like the happiness by the small river of my childhood, in a park whose oaks and lindens were to be cut down by the will of barbarous conquerors.

I bless you, rivers, I pronounce your names in the way my mother pronounced them, with respect yet tenderly.

Who will dare to say: I was called and that's the reason Might protected me from bullets ripping up the sand close by me, or drawing patterns on the wall above my head.

From a casual arrest just for elucidating the case, which would end with a journey in a freight car to a place from which the living do not return?

From obeying the order to register, when only the disobedient would survive?

Yes, but what about them, has not every one of them prayed to his God, begging: Save me!

And the sun was rising over camps of torture and even now with their eyes I see it rising.

I reach eighty, I fly from San Francisco to Frankfurt and Rome, a passenger who once traveled three days by horse carriage from Szetejnie to Wilno.

I fly Lufthansa, how nice that stewardess is, all of them are so civilized that it would be tactless to remember who they were.

On Capri a rejoicing and banqueting humanity invites me to take part in the festivity of incessant renewal.

Naked arms of women, a hand driving a bow across the strings, among evening gowns, glares and flashes open for me a moment of assent to the frivolity of our species.

They do not need a belief in Heaven and Hell, labyrinths of philosophy, mortification of the flesh by fasting.

And yet they are afraid of a sign that the unavoidable is close: a tumor in the breast, blood in the urine, high blood pressure.

Then they know for certain that all of us are called, and each of us meditates on the extravagance of having a separate fate.

Together with my epoch I go away, prepared for a verdict that will count me among its phantoms.

If I accomplished anything, it was only when I, a pious boy, chased after the disguises of the lost Reality.

After the real presence of divinity in our flesh and blood which are at the same time bread and wine,

Hearing the immense call of the Particular, despite the earthly law that sentences memory to extinction.

A CERTAIN NEIGHBORHOOD

I told nobody I was familiar with that neighborhood.
Why should I? As if a hunter with a spear
Materialized, looking for something he once knew.
After many incarnations we return to the earth,
Uncertain we would recognize its face.
Where there were villages and orchards, now nothing, fields.
Instead of old timber, young groves,
The level of the waters is lower, the swamp disappeared
Together with the scent of *ledum,* black grouse, and adders.
A little river should be here. Yes, but hidden in the brush,
Not, as before, amidst meadows. And the two ponds
Must have covered themselves with duckweed
Before they sank into black loam.
The glitter of a small lake, but its shores lack the rushes
Through which we struggled forward, swimming,
To dry ourselves afterwards, I and Miss X, and one towel, dancing.

A MEADOW

It was a riverside meadow, lush, from before the hay harvest,
On an immaculate day in the sun of June.
I searched for it, found it, recognized it.
Grasses and flowers grew there familiar in my childhood.
With half-closed eyelids I absorbed luminescence.
And the scent garnered me, all knowing ceased.
Suddenly I felt I was disappearing and weeping with joy.

REALISM

We are not so badly off, if we can
Admire Dutch painting. For that means
We shrug off what we have been told
For a hundred, two hundred years. Though we lost
Much of our previous confidence. Now we agree
That those trees outside the window, which probably exist,
Only pretend to greenness and treeness
And that language loses when it tries to cope
With clusters of molecules. And yet, this here:
A jar, a tin plate, a half-peeled lemon,
Walnuts, a loaf of bread, last—and so strongly
It is hard not to believe in their lastingness.
And thus abstract art is brought to shame,
Even if we do not deserve any other.
Therefore I enter those landscapes
Under a cloudy sky from which a ray
Shoots out, and in the middle of dark plains
A spot of brightness glows. Or the shore
With huts, boats, and on yellowish ice
Tiny figures skating. All this
Is here eternally, just because, once, it was.
Splendor (certainly incomprehensible)
Touches a cracked wall, a refuse heap,
The floor of an inn, jerkins of the rustics,
A broom, and two fish bleeding on a board.
Rejoice! Give thanks! I raised my voice
To join them in their choral singing,
Amid their ruffles, collets, and silk skirts,
Already one of them, who vanished long ago.
And our song soared up like smoke from a censer.

HOUSE IN KRASNOGRUDA

I
The woods reached water and there was immense silence.
A crested grebe popped up on the surface of the lake,
In deep water, very still, a flock of teals.
That's what was seen by a man on the shore
Who decided to build his house here
And to cut down the primeval oak forest.
He was thinking of timber he would float down the Niemen
And of thalers he would count by candlelight.

II
The ash trees in the park calmed down after the storm.
The young lady runs down a path to the lake.
She pulls her dress over her head
(She does not wear panties though Mademoiselle gets angry),
And there is a delight in the water's soft touch
When she swims, dog-style, self-taught,
Toward brightness, beyond the shade of the trees.

III
The company settles into a boat, ladies and gentlemen
In swimming suits. Just as they will be remembered
By a frail boy whose lifeline is short.
In the evening he learns to dance the tango. Mrs. Irena
Leads him, with that smirk of a mature woman
Who initiates a young male.
Out the door to the veranda owls are hooting.

TO MRS. PROFESSOR IN DEFENSE OF
MY CAT'S HONOR AND NOT ONLY

My valiant helper, a small-sized tiger
Sleeps sweetly on my desk, by the computer,
Unaware that you insult his tribe.

Cats play with a mouse or with a half-dead mole.
You are wrong, though: it's not out of cruelty.
They simply like a thing that moves.

For, after all, we know that only consciousness
Can for a moment move into the Other,
Empathize with the pain and panic of a mouse.

And such as cats are, all of Nature is.
Indifferent, alas, to the good and the evil.
Quite a problem for us, I am afraid.

Natural history has its museums,
But why should our children learn about monsters,
An earth of snakes and reptiles for millions of years?

Nature devouring, nature devoured,
Butchery day and night smoking with blood.
And who created it? Was it the good Lord?

Yes, undoubtedly, they are innocent,
Spiders, mantises, sharks, pythons.
We are the only one who say: cruelty.

Our consciousness and our conscience
Alone in the pale anthill of galaxies
Put their hope in a humane God.

Who cannot but feel and think,
Who is kindred to us by his warmth and movement,
For we are, as he told us, similar to Him.

Yet if it is so, then He takes pity
On every mauled mouse, every wounded bird.
Then the universe for him is like a Crucifixion.

Such is the outcome of your attack on the cat:
A theological, Augustinian grimace,
Which makes difficult our walking on this earth.

THIS WORLD

It appears that it was all a misunderstanding.
What was only a trial run was taken seriously.
The rivers will return to their beginnings.
The wind will cease in its turning about.
Trees instead of budding will tend to their roots.
Old men will chase a ball, a glance in the mirror—
They are children again.
The dead will wake up, not comprehending.
Till everything that happened has unhappened.
What a relief! Breathe freely, you who suffered much.

IN SZETEJNIE

You were my beginning and again I am with you, here, where I learned the four quarters of the globe.

Below, behind the trees, the River's quarter; to the back, behind the buildings, the quarter of the Forest; to the right, the quarter of the Holy Ford; to the left, the quarter of the Smithy and the Ferry.

Wherever I wandered, through whatever continents, my face was always turned to the River.

Feeling in my mouth the taste and the scent of the rosewhite flesh of calamus.

Hearing old pagan songs of harvesters returning from the fields, while the sun on quiet evenings was dying out behind the hills.

In the greenery gone wild I could still locate the place of an arbor where you forced me to draw my first awkward letters.

And I would try to escape to my hideouts, for I was certain that I would never learn how to write.

I did not expect, either, to learn that though bones fall into dust, and dozens of years pass, there is still the same presence.

That we could, as we do, live in the realm of eternal mirrors, working our way at the same time through unmowed grasses.

II

You held the reins and we were riding, you and me, in a one-horse britzka, for a visit to the big village by the forest.

The branches of its apple trees and pear trees were bowed down under the weight of fruits, ornate carved porches stood out above little gardens of mallow and rue.

Your former pupils, now farmers, entertained us with talks of crops, women showed their looms and deliberated with you about the colors of the warp and the woof.

On the table slices of ham and sausage, a honeycomb in a clay bowl, and I was drinking *kvas* from a tin cup.

I asked the director of the collective farm to show me that village; he took me to fields empty up to the edge of the forest, stopping the car before a huge boulder.

"Here was the village Peiksva" he said, not without triumph in his voice, as is usual with those on the winning side.

I noticed that one part of the boulder was hacked away, somebody had tried to smash the stone with a hammer, so that not even that trace might remain.

III

I ran out in a summer dawn into the voices of the birds, and I returned, but between the two moments I created my work.

Even though it was so difficult to pull up the stick of *n,* so it joined the stick of *u* or to dare building a bridge between *r* and *z.*

I kept a reedlike penholder and dipped its nib in the ink, a wandering scribe, with an ink pot at his belt.

Now I think one's work stands in the stead of happiness and becomes twisted by horror and pity.

Yet the spirit of this place must be contained in my work, just as it is contained in you who were led by it since childhood.

Garlands of oak leaves, the ave-bell calling for the May service, I wanted to be good and not to walk among the sinners.

But now when I try to remember how it was, there is only a pit, and it's so dark, I cannot understand a thing.

All we know is that sin exists and punishment exists, whatever philosophers would like us to believe.

If only my work were of use to people and of more weight than is my evil.

You alone, wise and just, would know how to calm me, explaining that I did as much as I could.

That the gate of the Black Garden closes, peace, peace, what is finished is finished.

WATERING CAN

Of a green color, standing in a shed alongside rakes and spades, it comes alive when it is filled with water from the pond, and an abundant shower pours from its nozzle, in an act, we feel it, of charity toward plants. It is not certain, however, that the watering can would have such a place in our memory, were it not for our training in noticing things. For, after all, we have been trained. Our painters do not often imitate the Dutch, who liked to paint still lifes, and yet photography contributes to our paying attention to detail and the cinema taught us that objects, once they appear on the screen, would participate in the actions of the characters and therefore should be noticed. There are also museums where canvases glorify not only human figures and landscapes but also a multitude of objects. The watering can has thus a good chance of occupying a sizable place in our imagination, and, who knows, perhaps precisely in this, in our clinging to distinctly delineated shapes, does our hope reside, of salvation from the turbulent waters of nothingness and chaos.

FROM MY DENTIST'S WINDOW

Extraordinary. A house. Tall. Surrounded by air. It stands. In the middle of a blue sky.

AFTER

Convictions, beliefs, opinions,
certainties, principles,
rules and habits have abandoned me.

I woke up naked at the edge of a civilization
which seemed to me comic and incomprehensible.

The vaulted halls of the post-Jesuit academy
where I had taken my classes
would not have been pleased with me.

Though I preserved a few sentences in Latin.

The river flows through a forest of oak and pine.

I stand in grass up to my waist,
Breathing in the wild scent of yellow flowers.

Above, white clouds. As is usual in my district,
an abundance of white clouds.

By the river Wilia, 1999

MY GRANDFATHER
SIGISMUND KUNAT

In the photograph of my grandfather Kunat when he was six is contained, in my opinion, the secret of his personality.

A happy little boy, youthful and sprightly, the bright and serene soul visible through his skin.

The photograph comes from the 1860s, and now I, in my old age, join that child at his play.

By a familiar lake into which he is now throwing pebbles, under ash trees that were to find their way into my poems.

The Kunats were ranked with the Calvinist gentry, which I snobbishly note down, since in our Lithuania Calvinists were counted among the most enlightened.

The family changed their denomination to Roman Catholic late, around 1800, yet I have not preserved any image of my grandfather in a pew at Swiętobrość.

He never spoke evil of priests, though, nor departed in anything from accepted norms of behavior.

A student at the Main School in Warsaw, he danced at balls and studied the books of the epoch of positivism.

He took seriously calls for "organic work" and for that reason established in Szetejnie a workshop for the manufacture of cloth, which is why I used to play in rooms crowded with presses for fulling.

He was exquisitely polite to everyone, great and small, rich and poor, and had the gift of listening with attention to everyone.

Oscar Milosz, who met him in Kaunas in 1922, called him *"un gentil-homme français du dixhuitième siècle,"* a French gentleman of the eighteenth century.

This external polish did not tell the whole story; underneath he was hiding wisdom and genuine goodness.

Meditating on my hereditary flaws, I have moments of relief any time I think of my grandfather; I had to have taken something from him, so I cannot be completely worthless.

He was called a "Lithuanizer," and did he not build a school in Legmedis and pay for a Lithuanian teacher?

Everyone liked him, Poles, Lithuanians and Jews, he was held in esteem by neighboring villages—

Those villages which were, a few years after his death, deported to Siberia, so that now in their place there is only an empty plain.

Among all books he liked best the memoirs of Jalub Gieysztor, for they described in detail our valley of Niewiaza between Kiejdany and Krakinowo.

They did not interest me in my youth; all my attention was directed toward the future.

Now I read those memoirs avidly, for I have learned the value of the names of localities, turns in the road, hills, and ferries on the river.

How much one must appreciate the province, the home and dates and traces of bygone people.

A Californian wanderer, I have kept a talisman: a photograph of the hill in Swiętobrość where, under the oaks, my grandfather Kunat is buried, and my great-grandfather Szymon Syruc, and his wife, Eufrozyna.

WHAT I LEARNED FROM JEANNE HERSCH

1. That reason is a gift of God and that we should believe in its ability to comprehend the world.

2. That they have been wrong who undermined our confidence in reason by enumerating the forces that want to usurp it: class struggle, libido, will to power.

3. That we should be aware that our being is enclosed within the circle of its perceptions, but not reduce reality to dreams and the phantoms of the mind.

4. That truth is a proof of freedom and that the sign of slavery is the lie.

5. That the proper attitude toward being is respect and that we must, therefore, avoid the company of people who debase being with their sarcasm, and praise nothingness.

6. That, even if we are accused of arrogance, it is the case that in the life of the mind a strict hierarchy is mandatory.

7. That intellectuals in the twentieth century were afflicted with the habit of *baratin,* i.e., irresponsible jabber.

8. That in the hierarchy of human activities the arts stand higher than philosophy, and yet bad philosophy can spoil art.

9. That objective truth exists; namely, out of two contrary assertions, one is true, one false, except in strictly defined cases when maintaining contradiction is legitimate.

10. That quite independently of the fate of religious denominations we should preserve a "philosophical faith," i.e., a belief in transcendence as a measure of humanity.

11. That time excludes and sentences to oblivion only those works of our hands and minds which prove worthless in raising up, century after century, the huge edifice of civilization.

12. That in our lives we should not succumb to despair because of our errors and our sins, for the past is never closed down and receives the meaning we give it by our subsequent acts.

PASTELS BY DEGAS

That shoulder. An erotic thing submerged in duration.
Her hands are entangled in undone plaits of red hair
So dense that, combed, it pulls, the head down,
A thigh, and under it the foot of another leg.
For she is sitting, her bent knees open,
And the movement of her arm reveals the shape of a breast.
Here undoubtedly. In a century, a year
That have vanished entirely. How to reach her?
And how to reach the other in her yellow robe?
She puts on mascara, humming a song.
The third lies on the bed, smokes a cigarette,
And looks through a fashion journal. Her muslin shirt
Shows a white roundness and pinkish nipples.
The painter's hat hangs on the entresol
With their dresses. He liked to stay here, chatting,
Sketching. Our human communion has a bitter taste
Because of the familiarity of touch, of avid lips,
The shape of loins, and talk of an immortal soul.
It flows and recedes. A wave, a sighing of surf.
And only a red mane flickered in the abyss.

UNDE MALUM

Where does evil come from?
It comes

from man
always from man
only from man

—Tadeusz Rozewicz

Alas, dear Tadeusz,
good nature and wicked man
are romantic inventions
you show us this way
the depth of your optimism

so let man exterminate
his own species
the innocent sunrise will illuminate
a liberated flora and fauna

where oak forests reclaim
the postindustrial wasteland
and the blood of a deer
torn asunder by a pack of wolves
is not seen by anyone
a hawk falls upon a hare
without witness
evil disappears from the world
and consciousness with it

Of course, dear Tadeusz,
evil (and good) comes from man.

RAYS OF DAZZLING LIGHT

Light off metal shaken,
Lucid dew of heaven,
Bless each and every one
To whom the earth is given.

Its essence was always hidden
Behind a distant curtain.
We chased it all our lives
Bidden and unbidden.

Knowing the hunt would end,
That then what had been rent
Would be at last made whole:
Poor body and the soul.

LATE RIPENESS

Not soon, as late as the approach of my ninetieth year,
I felt a door opening in me and I entered
the clarity of early morning.

One after another my former lives were departing,
like ships, together with their sorrow.

And the countries, cities, gardens, the bays of seas
assigned to my brush came closer,
ready now to be described better than they were before.

I was not separated from people,
grief and pity joined us.
We forget—I kept saying—that we are all children of the King.

For where we come from there is no division
into Yes and No, into is, was, and will be.

We were miserable, we used no more than a hundredth part
of the gift we received for our long journey.

Moments from yesterday and from centuries ago—
a sword blow, the painting of eyelashes before a mirror
of polished metal, a lethal musket shot, a caravel
staving its hull against a reef—they dwell in us,
waiting for a fulfillment.

I knew, always, that I would be a worker in the vineyard,
as are all men and women living at the same time,
whether they are aware of it or not.

IF THERE IS NO GOD

If there is no God,
Not everything is permitted to man.
He is still his brother's keeper
And he is not permitted to sadden his brother,
By saying that there is no God.

CLASSMATE

I was walking toward her, carrying a half-opened rose.
I was riding, because it was a long journey.

Through a labyrinth of escalators, from a pit to a pit,
In the company of several phantasmagoric ladies.

She was reclining on a carpet, receiving guests,
Her neck a lily of immaculate whiteness.

Please kneel here, she said, next to me,
We are going to talk about the good and the beautiful.

She was reclining, produced graphomaniac poems.
This happened in another country, in a lost century.

She used to wear a student cap adorned with wolf's teeth,
An emblem of our alma mater sewn into the velvet.

No doubt she married, had three children.
Who can track down these details?

Does the dream mean I desired her?
Or just felt pity for her former body?

So that it falls to me to count her scattered bones
Since I am the last from among that gang of youths from a century
    past?

A descent into a Dantesque dark hollow
Somewhere near Archangel or in Kazakhstan?

She should have been buried in the cemetery at Rossa,
But an evil fate no doubt carried her out of town.

Why her precisely, I don't understand.
I'm not sure I'd recognize her on a busy street.

And I ask myself why it is constructed so perversely;
So that life is vague and only death is real.

Farewell Piorewiczowna, unasked-for shadow.
I don't even remember your first name.

HIGH TERRACES

Terraces high above the brightness of the sea.
We were the first in the hotel to go down to breakfast.
Far off, on the horizon, huge ships maneuvered.

In King Sigismund Augustus High School
We used to begin each day with a song about dawn.

> *I wake to light that warms*
> *My eye*
> *And feel Almighty God*
> *Nearby.*

All my life I tried to answer the question, where does evil come from?
Impossible that people should suffer so much, if God is in Heaven
And nearby.

NOTEBOOK

To express. Noting can be expressed.
Fire under a stove lid. Anastasia is making pancakes.
December. Before dawn. In a village near Jazuny.

✣

I should be dead already, but there is work to do.

✣

From human speech to the muteness of verse, how far!

✣

It spreads out, the valley, signs, lights.

✣

The mild valley of those who are eternally alive.
They walk by green waters.
With red ink they draw on my breast
A heart and the signs of a kindly welcome.

✣

To praise. Only this has been left
To the one who ponders, slowly,
Misfortune upon misfortune and from which side they struck.

✣

People near me don't know how difficult it is to pretend that nothing
  happened, that everything is normal.

✣

I loved God with all my strength on the sandy roads that wound
  through forests.

✣

Where is the memory of those days that were your days on earth
And effectuated joy and pain and were for you the universe.

❧

Low, beneath, in darkness,
A table and on it a thick book
And a hand inscribing something . . .

❧

At the gate of Hell she stood, naked.

❧

I want to describe the world as Lucretius did.
Yet there have been too many complications of late.
And the words in the dictionary are too few.
So I just say of the world, like Galileo: and yet it moves.

❧

She slipped out of her panties, Lady Polixena.

❧

My love in the dream, a squirrel in a hazel bush.

❧

Cities! You have never been described.

❧

The grown-ups led the cortege, deep in their stupid conversations.

❧

The river Wilia flows, indifferent.

❧

Stricken with pity and loathing.

ORPHEUS AND EURYDICE

Standing on flagstones of the sidewalk at the entrance to Hades
Orpheus hunched in a gust of wind
That tore at his coat, rolled past in waves of fog,
Tossed the leaves of the trees. The headlights of cars
Flared and dimmed in each succeeding wave.

He stopped at the glass-paneled door, uncertain
Whether he was strong enough for that ultimate trial.

He remembered her words: "You are a good man."
He did not quite believe it. Lyric poets
Usually have—as he knew—cold hearts.
It is like a medical condition. Perfection in art
Is given in exchange for such an affliction.

Only her love warmed him, humanized him.
When he was with her, he thought differently about himself.
He could not fail her now, when she was dead.

He pushed open the door and found himself walking in a labyrinth,
Corridors, elevators. The livid light was not light but the dark of the
    earth.
Electronic dogs passed him noiselessly.
He descended many floors, a hundred, three hundred, down.

He was cold, aware that he was Nowhere.
Under thousands of frozen centuries,
On an ashy trace where generations had moldered,
In a kingdom that seemed to have no bottom and no end.

Thronging shadows surrounded him.
He recognized some of the faces.
He felt the rhythm of his blood.

He felt strongly his life with its guilt
And he was afraid to meet those to whom he had done harm.
But they had lost the ability to remember
And gave him only a glance, indifferent to all that.

For his defense he had a nine-stringed lyre.
He carried in it the music of the earth, against the abyss
That buries all of sound in silence.
He submitted to the music, yielded
To the dictation of a song, listening with rapt attention,
Became, like his lyre, its instrument.

Thus he arrived at the palace of the rulers of that land.
Persephone, in her garden of withered pear and apple trees,
Black, with naked branches and verrucose twigs,
Listened from the funereal amethyst of her throne.

He sang the brightness of mornings and green rivers,
He sang of smoking water in the rose-colored daybreaks,
Of colors: cinnabar, carmine, burnt sienna, blue,
Of the delight of swimming in the sea under marble cliffs,
Of feasting on a terrace above the tumult of a fishing port,
Of the tastes of wine, olive oil, almonds, mustard, salt.
Of the flight of the swallow, the falcon,
Of a dignified flock of pelicans above a bay,
Of the scent of an armful of lilacs in summer rain,
Of his having composed his words always against death
And of having made no rhyme in praise of nothingness.

I don't know—said the goddess—whether you loved her or
    not.
Yet you have come here to rescue her.
She will be returned to you. But there are conditions:

You are not permitted to speak to her, or on the journey back
To turn your head, even once, to assure yourself that she is behind
    you.

And so Hermes brought forth Eurydice.
Her face no longer hers, utterly gray,
Her eyelids lowered beneath the shade of her lashes.
She stepped rigidly, directed by the hand
Of her guide. Orpheus wanted so much
To call her name, to wake her from that sleep.
But he refrained, for he had accepted the conditions.

And so they set out. He first, and then, not right away,
The slap of the god's sandals and the light patter
Of her feet fettered by her robe, as if by a shroud.
A steep climbing path phosphorized
Out of darkness like the walls of a tunnel.
He would stop and listen. But then
They stopped, too, and the echo faded.
And when he began to walk the double tapping commenced again.
Sometimes it seemed closer, sometimes more distant.
Under his faith a doubt sprang up
And entwined him like cold bindweed.
Unable to weep, he wept at the loss
Of the human hope for the resurrection of the dead,
Because he was, now, like every other mortal.
His lyre was silent, yet he dreamed, defenseless.
He knew he must have faith and he could not have faith.
And so he would persist for a very long time,
Counting his steps in a half-wakeful torpor.

Day was breaking. Shapes of rock loomed up
Under the luminous eye of the exit from underground.

It happened as he expected. He turned his head
And behind him on the path was no one.

Sun. And sky. And in the sky white clouds.
Only now everything cried to him: Eurydice!
How will I live without you, my consoling one!
But there was a fragrant scent of herbs, the low humming of bees,
And he fell asleep with his cheek on the sun-warmed earth.

CZESLAW MILOSZ:
A BIOGRAPHICAL NOTE

C ZESLAW MILOSZ WAS BORN in the Lithuanian village of
Szetejnie, which lies in the valley of the Niewiaza River, in
1911. At that time most of Lithuania was a province of the
Russian Empire. Its culture was the culture of what had been the Grand
Duchy of Poland and Lithuania. Milosz has remarked that his grand-
parents' world was an eastern European version of the one we glimpse
in the novels of Thomas Hardy. It was a world of manor houses pre-
sided over by Polish gentry and worked by Lithuanian peasantry. Both
sets of Milosz's grandparents came from that gentry and both had a
mixed Polish-Lithuanian ancestry. His father was a military engineer in
the Czarist army, so as a young child Milosz traveled with his parents a
good deal. His prose recalls his wonder on seeing his first motorcar in
St. Petersburg on Nevsky Prospect; his poems remember travel on the
Trans-Siberian Express—its lush coupes and the bell that was rung to
call the passengers to meals—and the family story about a servant who
traveled with them and upon seeing the mountains of Siberia for the
first time, said, "Lord! They look like the Apostles!"

Milosz went to school in Wilno, as Vilnius was called in Polish, and
he returned there to go to high school and to the university. But dur-
ing summers, and in the years of the First World War, he and his mother
lived in the manor house of his grandparents near the village of Szetejnie,
some two hundred kilometers north of Wilno. I'm told that one could
walk down to the river from Milosz's grandfather's estate, get into a boat,
and float downriver to Wilno in about three hours.

Within the circle of this world—the gentry in the country and
ordinary working people in the cities—those who were not Jewish,
spoke Polish. The country people, if they were not Jewish, spoke Lith-
uanian. Among Jews the language of the lower classes and the country

people was Yiddish. Upper-class Jews spoke Russian. Polish was spoken in Milosz's grandparents' house and his parents spoke Polish at home, but to quote his account of the matter, "there was a strong influx of Russian because my father and the people who visited us in Wilno were fond of switching to Russian when the subject was humorous, something Poles are known to do.... I was under the sway of the Russian language until the spring of 1918. I was bilingual. I didn't have much of an idea why I spoke one language to some people and the other one to other people.... I used to play with two children, Yashka and Sonka, who lived in our courtyard in Wilno. They were from a Jewish family and they spoke Russian rather than Yiddish. Playing with them gave me practice with my Russian."

His mother, he has remarked, ran an elementary school founded in the spirit of "positivism and organic work," a sort of nineteenth century Montessori school that was charitably funded to teach poor Lithuanian children to read and write in Polish. Milosz reports that when he began school, though the pronunciation of Polish by the Lithuanian gentry was—and still is—the upper-class standard, his papers would come back with sentences underlined in red ink because his Polish was so full of expressions that his teachers considered regional curiosities—Russian, Lithuanian, Yiddish, and Belorussian borrowings that belonged quite naturally to his speech. He also began to learn French in grammar school, and his first attempts at writing poetry in Polish came from schoolboy translations of Ovid from the Latin.

In 1918, when Milosz was seven years old, a pretty, older cousin came to visit, and she began to read him one of the novels of Henry Sienkiewicz. Milosz described the event as an initiation. It was the moment when he entered the enchantment of the language that would take him through his early poems of the 1930s, with their turbulence and prophetic violence. These poems were written when he was a college student in Wilno/Vilnius. For a young writer, Wilno was the city of the romantic origins of Polish poetry. Adam Mickiewicz, the Pushkin of Polish poetry (who was also in his time a political exile), had gone to the university and so had Juliusz Slowacki, the Shelley or Keats of Polish romanticism.

Vilnius is the city Milosz remembers in his poem of exile, "City Without a Name," and the place where, with a group of poets who called themselves "Catastrophists," he published his first books. In this volume, "Song" and "Slow Rivers" will give readers a sense of his writing in that period. It was during this time also that Milosz visited Paris for the first time and was introduced to French literary society by his uncle, the Lithuanian-born French poet Oscar Milosz. In the midst of the Depression, he explored the city to which he would return first as a middle-level Communist diplomat and where, for ten years, he would survive as a freelance writer and something of an outcast in the pro-Communist milieu of French literary life.

World War II took him from Wilno to Warsaw, where he worked in public radio as a writer and then, after the German occupation, as a teamster carting books for the university library. He continued to write poems and edited several underground anthologies of poetry, including one called *Invincible Song*. He also translated and distributed through clandestine publishers an essay by the French philosopher Jacques Maritain on resistance to the Nazi regime. Milosz began to study English (his fifth or sixth language), reading Shakespeare and the poems of William Blake and T. S. Eliot. In Washington, as a cultural attaché to the Polish Embassy after the war, his English got put to use and he was able to improve it by reading the *Partisan Review* and, in Polish, summarizing its contents by way of supplying "briefings" on American culture to the home office. By the 1950s, he was an exile in Paris, living off the French he had first learned at school. In Paris, he wrote *The Captive Mind*, the book that made his international reputation; the prose books that began to look back to the world of his childhood; a novel, *The Issa Valley;* and a work of autobiography, *Native Realm.*

It was English that he brought with him to California. He lived on a hillside overlooking San Francisco Bay in Berkeley, and it was here where he wrote poems in Polish for another forty years. During that time he improved his Greek and worked up some Hebrew so he could translate the psalms of David into Polish. It was also in Berkeley where, toward the end of his life, he hired a tutor to help him improve what remained of his childhood Lithuanian. He told his friends that he wanted to be fluent in case Lithuanian turned out to be the language spoken in Heaven.

He got to return to Poland after the fall of the Communist regime in 1989 and then to Lithuania and to the riverbank of his childhood a few years later, after the collapse of the Soviet Union. It was a very remarkable closing of the circle of his life, one that had seemed inconceivable during his many years of exile and travel. In his last years he and his American second wife, Carol, lived in Krakow. They had a beautiful, old, high-ceilinged apartment just off the city's main square, which was frequented by the young Polish poets who gathered around him. Although English was his language at home, he was finally returned to the sounds of the Polish language in all its living forms. After his wife died unexpectedly, and rather cruelly—she was so much younger than he and they were so happy together—he was alone with Polish again. He said to friends, in the difficult days after her death, that he was surviving by incantation. One of the forms that incantation took was an elegy to his wife framed as a retelling of the story of Orpheus and Eurydice, the myth that he had read in Ovid as a schoolboy.

Milosz was buried in August 2004 after a high funeral Mass in the Basilica of St. Mary in the great square in Krakow, which was filled with thousands of his admirers. The altar and the casket were heaped with calamus and wild ginger—the white flowers of the Lithuanian summer—and after the funeral, at the graveside service, under a chestnut tree in the courtyard of the Church of St. Peter of the Rock, a part of his poem, "In Szetejnie," was read in Polish, Russian, Lithuanian, English, French, and Hebrew by his poet friends. It was written when he returned to Lithuania after leaving it fifty-one years earlier. It's a poem, appropriately enough, about learning how to write, and it's addressed to his mother:

IN SZETEJNIE

You were my beginning and again I am with you, here, where I learned the four quarters of the globe.

Below, behind the trees, the River's quarter; to the back, behind the buildings, the quarter of the Forest; to the right, the quarter of the Holy Ford; to the left, the quarter of the Smithy and the Ferry.

Wherever I wandered, through whatever continents, my face was always turned to the River.

Feeling in my mouth the taste and the scent of the rosewhite flesh of calamus.

Hearing old pagan songs of the harvesters returning from the fields, while the sun on quiet evenings was dying out behind the hills.

In the greenery gone wild I could still locate the place of an arbor where you forced me to draw my first awkward letters.

And I would try to escape to my hideouts, for I was certain that I would never learn how to write.

I did not expect, either, to learn that though bones fall into dust, and dozens of years pass, there is still the same presence.

That we could, as we do, live in the realm of eternal mirrors, working our way at the same time through unmowed grasses.

INDEX OF POEMS AND TRANSLATORS

The poems were translated by Czeslaw Milosz and Robert Hass, except as initialed.